Dark Waters

Vol. I

Dark Waters

Vol. I

Contents

For a list of trigger warnings, please see pg 193

Introduction

It's the fall of 2020.

I'm sitting in a terribly uncomfortable office chair at a terribly uncomfortable desk at my apartment in South Harlem with a very, very strong drink and N.B. Turner on the phone. We're watching a webcast of a writers event that's supposed to touch on query letters "from every genre."

There is no horror, no noir, no crime. Nothing gritty. Nothing scary.

And I, with all the bravado whisky and quarantine can give a person say, "We should just do this ourselves."

To my incredible surprise, he agrees. He jumps at it. He says, no, really, we should do this.

And how can I adequately explain what that agreement has done?

Dark Waters started as a concept of how to promote indie authors. It began more on the side of editing, reading stories/works in progress and going through thoughts on how to edit them, to get them in the best possible shape for submission, to give the work the best chance possible for acceptance. Three years later, over 50 episodes, hours of laughter and conversation later, and we've learned…. a lot. We're getting better at what we do. Our format has shifted to focus on author interviews and 'book club' reviews. We're getting braver in reaching out to authors. We've been to conventions. We've done readings, had our work published, met some absolutely fantastic people.

But when it came time to work on the website, the best moments I had uploading our old content was listing on quite a few of our beginning episodes, "*This piece has now been published in.....*"

To get to say that stories we'd had in rough draft versions on our show have since been published? That felt pretty damn good. It still feels pretty damn good.

It's kind of insane to look back on how far we've grown the past couple of years. Since we started the show, we've both been given some incredible opportunities. He's now editor-in-chief of *Hooiser Noir*. I somehow convinced a press to release my first book. But in a way, it makes absolute sense that we've come almost full circle to what we originally said we would do – give some amazing writers a chance to share their words. This time, now in print.

I am always and forever grateful for N.B.'s support on this wild experiment we've been on; for the friendship that has only grown on every twist and turn we've been through together with the show.

Thank you to everyone who has been on, listened to, or shared our show. This book exists because of you. We've only gotten to do the show this long, with plans to keep growing and getting better and better, because of you. You're awesome, and you should know it.

For all the authors in this book, thank you so, so much for submitting to us. For trusting us. For your incredible words and immense talent.

But, most importantly, thank you, dear reader, for picking up this book of wonderfully dark stories. For believing that dark fiction deserves to exist in dark times. For supporting indie authors and indie presses. For being willing to dive into unknown, treacherous waters, to see what's on the other side.

With all the gratitude this icy heart can muster,

Kirstyn

We had no idea how this project would work. We had some drunken text messages, a few friends with some stories and some time, and a poor understanding of how to produce good quality audio recordings. We recorded the first episode three separate times before we thought it was good enough to release. By all rights, the Dark Waters Podcast was a shot in the dark, and at the start, we didn't yet know what target we were trying to hit.

Three years, numerous guests, a novel, and multiple publications later, we've now found ourselves able to publish an anthology of stories we love and are honored to share with you all.

This journey is a labor of love for the two of us: love for stories, for people, for the tangential conversations which result in laughter and understanding and really bad dad jokes. And more than anything, apart from getting to share this with a dear friend, the best part of it all for me is knowing that you all have chosen to come along for the ride. For a couple geeks who met in high school who somehow ended up feeling like the cool kids (well, Kirstyn is cool, I'm just the half-decent comic relief), it means more than you could know.

To those who listen and share, thank you so much for giving us your time and letting us talk your ears off.

To those who have published our work and the work of our guests, thank you for giving space to good storytelling and beautiful things.

To our guests, thank you for trusting us with your work and your stories and your ideas.

And to those who bought this anthology, thank you for jumping in the deep end of the water. There's a lot to find here, and it only gets better the deeper you go. Just remember to always look beneath the surface.

In humor, in gratitude, in hope for the future, and love for you all,

N.B. Turner

pinkest pink

Jacob Close

There were no words for the horror contained within that little square of pink paper. Unnamed and unknown, having not yet been born, but gestating. Developing, somewhere between fuchsia and blush.

Pickman tapped the swatch with a well-manicured finger, and the sides of his lips curled into a conspiratorial smirk.

"What do you think?" he asked.

Miles squinted at it. The gallery office's glass walls and harsh overhead bulbs peppered the glossy paper with mildewy spots of light, giving the already oversaturated sample an appearance not unlike an oncoming headache.

When he could take no more Miles leaned back into his chair again, took a moment to fix his posture, and slid Pickman a diplomatic grimace.

"It's nice. Good, I mean."

"Let's not play the diplomat, Mister Warren," Pickman replied. "It's shit. Utter horseshit, *you* know it, *I* know it."

With a single deft movement Pickman crushed the glossy paper between his thumb and forefinger, as easily and spitefully as one might crush an ant. That sort of confidence made Miles Warren envious. Perhaps even jealous. Whatever it took to so casually wreck a five-thousand-dollar pigment sample, be it the self-assurance of genius or an idiot's confidence, he wanted it.

"It's been the same story since they invented Vantablack: pasty little philistines in pale little lab coats, calling a test tube a picture frame. The media eats it up, of course - my man at the Telegraph says they're going to name it 'prime blush', whatever the hell that means," Pickman continued, pausing briefly to take a sip of espresso. "They send it out with a little dossier of numbers and figures attached. Spectroscopy this, luminance value that. It's like reading over a cancer diagnosis."

Miles glanced at the crumpled sample on the ground. Against the pale white tiles of Pickman's office it seemed to insist itself upon his peripherals, lingering like a chemical smell at the edge of his senses.

"So… you want me to recreate it?" he ventured, finally bringing his eyes up. Pickman let out a chuckle and shook his head.

"No, Mister Warren," he replied. "I want you to utterly destroy them."

The conversation lulled for a few moments as Pickman picked a pack of cigarettes from his suit pocket, an all-black Turkish brand that was likely too expensive for Miles to recognize. Behind him, London's jagged slate spires jostled for space in the wraparound window, austere against a smoke-toned sky. Privately Miles imagined what it must be like to have that view every day. A view so much unlike his own, despite being the same city.

Before he could ruminate too much on the thought, however, Pickman floated back to the foreground on a cloud of fossil-coloured smoke.

"I'll cut to the chase: I attended your exhibition at Granary Square and I liked what I saw. Artists who mix their own pigments are a rarity these days, and your command of colour – if a little derivative of Matisse – is breathtaking."

"Thank you."

"I'm planning an exhibition in answer to this *prime blush* nonsense on July 18th. A shade far in excess of their pitiful little attempt, the pinkest pink ever made by man – or, more specifically, by you."

Miles felt himself go white. The crumpled sample on the floor reasserted itself again, this time with all the threat of a hot iron.

"That's…that's an incredible offer, Mister Pickman," Miles said, before trailing off. Beads of sweat were forming on his palms. "I just really wouldn't know where to start."

"Am I to take that as refusal?"

"No! No, I'm…I'm sure I could do it, but it would take time. More time than you're suggesting, certainly. A year, if not more."

"Three months is ample. I shall put you up in one of our studio apartments, provide you with whatever equipment or supplies you need within reason. All I need is a ten-by-ten canvas, unicolour, no need to overcomplicate it," Pickman explained, and a mischievous grin crept across his cheeks. "On the unveiling day, we'll have a patent officer officiate a declaration of inventorship before a live audience. Then, we'll burn it."

"*Burn* it?"

"Like a zen garden, Mister Warren. A moment's excess."

Pickman pointed through the glass walls towards the staircase, and presumably to the treasure trove waiting downstairs.

"In return, I would give you residency of the east wing for six months. All of it. Any new work you produce would have a place here, no questions asked. I'm sure I don't need to impress upon you the opportunities that would come with such exposure."

Miles gave Pickman a smile back, though neither man could tell whether it was borne of fear or desperate excitement. Both of them knew that no artist would pass up a chance to hang in the Pickman Gallery. People had made offers to pull out their own teeth for the privilege.

"So, can I assume you accept?" Pickman ventured.

Miles' eyes wandered a final time to the crumpled sample. It seemed a hundred feet tall now, and luminous as the sun. It made him think of his own dark, cramped apartment, and the many less desirable shades within; the dull red of dead LED indicators on the heating system, the ethereal blue of mouldy food, the unforgiving black-and-white of overdue bills arrayed like deconstructed skulls on a pale pine counter.

When faced with such terrible colours, what else could he do?

‡

The 18th of June arrived in grey company. The cloud cover which had lingered on from a morose spring remained overhead, drabness inside and out. Pickman sat at his desk, not doing anything. Just waiting, like a lion in its den.

The glass door creaked open, and a young woman shuffled inside – the latest of a never-ending parade of interns destined to burn out, bend over a desk or 'find another passion' pointedly outside the industry. They'd be invisible to Pickman if not for the name tags which, ultimately, were more for the benefit of their dignity than his interest. This one's name was Natalie, apparently.

"Sir?" she said, clutching her clipboard close. "Mister Warren's waiting in the foyer."

"Send him in."

She disappeared with a merciful lack of small talk and reappeared a few minutes later, flanking a decidedly grey Miles Warren. He lingered outside the glass door for a moment as if Pickman couldn't see him, shoulders slumped in defeat like a man going to an execution, which seemed a good sign – it let Pickman know exactly where the lines of battle and surrender were drawn. He waved them both in, Miles sitting heavily down on the seat opposite and Natalie hovering silently in the far corner.

"Good afternoon," said Pickman, adding, "though I might have preferred good morning."

"I'm sorry I'm late. I've not been sleeping well... what am I saying, that's not your problem," Miles apologised, looking around at the room with hollow eyes, as if it were the first time he'd seen it. Then he startled abruptly, remembering the briefcase still clamped in his grip. "I have the latest drafts here. Number, ah... I think it's numbers eighty-one or eighty-two through one hundred."

"I see."

The conversation stopped briefly and Miles squirmed in his chair, as if his skin were too tight and too itchy, while Pickman stubbed out his cigarette to light a new one - if only to let the dread hang awhile longer. Too many people got into the art world for the prestige or the aesthetic, but Pickman was in it mostly for the inevitable silences: the kind of quiet which had a winner and a loser, and to which he was seldom on the latter side.

"Go on, then," he said eventually.

Miles opened the briefcase with shaking hands and a collection of coloured squares spilled over the glass table. All pink, some deeper and some lighter, in shades from hot desire to half-hearted longing. Pickman took them up one by one, examining each with the clinical displeasure of a surgeon, turning it in the light to ascertain tone, depth, luminescence.

All the while Miles watched in silence, visibly on the brink of tears, until finally he could take no more.

"What do you think?" he whispered.

"This one," Pickman replied without looking up at him. "Explain it."

Miles cleared his throat.

"That's a 3:2:1 ratio of calcium, tin and silicon oxides mixed with rubia tinctorum extract."

Pickman curled his lip and threw the sample aside. Miles' eyes visibly tracked

the piece of paper down to the ground, and the moment it hit the tile he slumped as if struck.

"What a waste of good chemicals," Pickman said.

Miles held his head in his hands and muttered something that sounded like an apology, and Pickman leaned back in his chair.

Slowly, calmly, he steepled his fingers together, cigarette hanging loosely from between thin lips.

"This is our fourth unsuccessful meeting, Mister Warren. A less charitable man might begin to think you're doing this on purpose."

"I'm not."

"Then why am I forced to contend with this *constant* parade of mediocrity?" Pickman insisted, holding up one of the samples. "Look at this. I wouldn't put this in a child's playroom let alone a gallery, what the hell were you thinking?"

"I was-"

"One month, Warren. That's all. That's *it*. In a months' time the most influential critics and curators in London are going to piled into that room downstairs, waiting to see what you've done. And if you give them *this*," he said, waving another sample, "I can guarantee you'll never work again. Not in London, not anywhere. Is that what you want?"

Abruptly, Miles began to weep. It was a pathetic sight, a grown man with his face buried in his palms, sucking breaths through the gaps in tear-slick fingers. Pickman watched it dispassionately, waiting until the increasingly frantic sobbing reached its apex and extinguished into a low, panicked mewling.

"I'm sorry," Miles murmured, over and over again. Pickman pushed the empty briefcase back across the table.

"Get out," he said, pointing to the door. "Come back in two weeks, and for God's sake stop embarrassing yourself like this."

Miles let out a final, half-strangled noise before he left, biting his lip hard to try and kill it mid-sob. Then he sloped from the glass office and out the door, descending the stairs to the gallery like a man shell-shocked; every step a surprise, and a torment. Pickman watched him crawl out of sight before turning his attention to the other presence in the room: Natalie, still stood in the corner as before, though now she stared at the floor in a visible attempt not to be included. That piqued Pickman's interest.

"I'm sure you've got something to say," he asked, and Natalie started as if stung.

"No, sir."

"Go on. I mean it, say what you'd like," he insisted. "You can curse at me, I won't mind. Anything to end this tiresome air of unspoken loathing you've had for the past week."

Natalie pursed her lips. Her deep brown eyes wandered towards the glass desk, and its accompanying drifts of pink.

"I thought they were good. That's all," she said curtly. Pickman considered the statement for a few seconds, then nodded as he re-lit his cigarette.

"Yes, they were."

Natalie blinked at him.

"I'm sorry?"

"You're right. They're good, better than almost any other pigment mixes I've seen before," Pickman casually opined, plucking a square up from the floor. "If Warren continues to push himself, I've no doubt these will be quite the collector's item down the line."

"Then why...?."

Pickman sighed. Then he stood up from his desk, and carefully buttoned his jacket.

"Follow me."

The storage area lay below the main floor of the gallery, but seemed a world away. Instead of the well-curated and intricately designed lights of the main floor, this underworld was bathed instead in the jaundiced glow of bare halogen bulbs, the floors clothed in dust, the air heavy with the scent of cobalt and gesso decaying in a mass tomb. Natalie followed Pickman down dutifully, wandering deeper and deeper into the intestines of the ancient building until finally they reached a back corner of the tunnel, where rows of sleeping artworks slumbered like corpses beneath their dust sheets. Without ceremony Pickman pulled away the cover from the largest of the paintings, then stepped back to admire it.

"This is his. Tell me what you think."

"It's beautiful," Natalie breathed, tottering back a few steps as she considered the wild cacophony of reds upon on the canvas. Pickman put his hands in his pockets and studied it too, allowing himself the briefest stirring of remembered awe in the process. A treat.

"He painted it nearly a decade ago, his last work before he burnt out like a match. Do you know what preceded it?"

Natalie shook her head.

"His father and mother died suddenly; a burglary gone wrong, or at least that's what the papers said. As I understand it, the intruder sawed their heads off while they were still in their pyjamas."

"Oh, god."

"Warren painted this piece two days later, then had a nervous breakdown after the exhibition at Granary Square. Nobody saw him for years after that."

Pickman reached forwards and brushed his fingers down the thick ridges of paint. In every stroke was an anguish so pure it was utterly elemental, dancing and howling and *clawing* itself with every swoop of ruby and claret crimson. Every hue was a revelation. Not reddest red, but close.

"Before the murders Miles Warren was nothing more than a second-rate O'Keefe, but this... When I saw it, I knew it had to be him. I knew what he was capable of, and I knew what it took to put him there. The world deserves to see that."

"Hasn't he been through enough, then? He's vulnerable, Mister Pickman, if he had a breakdown already-"

"No pearls without irritants," Pickman interrupted, cutting her off. "All I'm doing is applying pressure, nothing more. If Miles Warren needs mental anguish in order to reach his full potential, I'd say I'm doing both him and the art community a favour by inducing it."

Natalie finally looked away from the painting, brow cracked with wholly unveiled disgust.

"I think that's monstrous to do that to a person, Mister Pickman. Even for the sake of art."

Pickman narrowed his eyes at her. Then he took the fallen dust cover from the floor and covered the wall of red.

"Then quit," he said, walking back upstairs.

‡

The morning of July 1st turned quickly to afternoon, turned quickly to evening. Pickman waited impatiently in his office, staring through the wraparound window as the sky turned to fire. Eight hours late and counting.

And then, a knock on the door.

"Enter," Pickman said, lifting the wine glass to his lips rather than turn around. Clacking high-heel footsteps crept into the room.

"Mister Pickman?"

"Well? Did you go to the apartment?"

"I did, sir. He wasn't there, so I talked to a neighbour."

At that Pickman swivelled his seat, but rather than the expected face of apology he instead found himself confronted with a mask of accusation. An I-told-you-so writ large upon Natalie's brow, and in the darkly folded creases of her downturned lips.

"He's in the hospital. Where he's been for the last week, after an ambulance crew took him away," she said, expression finally cracking under the weight of her disdain. "He tried to kill himself on Sunday."

Pickman swirled the red wine in his glass, clicked his teeth, then took a long, slow sip.

"How?" he asked. Natalie brushed a few stray hairs from her face and tensed her jaw, as if having to rip each word away from a bungee cord in her throat.

"He went at himself with a knife. And then, for good measure? He drank paint thinner."

"I see."

"That's all? You *see*? You drove him to this—"

"Careful." Pickman insisted, raising a finger. "If you'd let me finish, I was going to ask you to go to the apartment and collect some personal items for him."

Natalie shifted uncomfortably, unbalanced by the unexpected turn. But still, tense indignance won out.

"I warned you about what you were doing," she said. Pickman frowned and took a sip of wine, his eyes hot coals. Not roused, yet burning all the same.

"I've said to you before: if you disagree with my methods, you know where the door is – your continued presence here suggests at least *some* level of willingness to be complicit. Whether it's for money or aspiration makes no difference, you're a whore to some great whim all the same," he growled. "Don't imagine yourself better than me. Don't forget where you are, and don't forget your place."

For a moment it looked as if Natalie might fight. But then, something invisible tugged her back. The hook of whatever got her up in the morning, pulling tight. Pickman would never know what it was that overcame her morals, nor did he care to. Everyone was desperate for something, after all.

She hung her head low. Clasped her hands.

"Sorry, Mister Pickman."

Pickman didn't respond. His attention, suddenly and silently, lay elsewhere.

They weren't alone.

Someone was stood in the vestibule. A shadow on the other side of the glass wall. The figure shambled closer and opened the door, face revealed abruptly by the change in light. Natalie turned and immediately let out a horrified yelp, clapping her palms over her mouth as she backed instinctively away. Pickman said nothing.

"I'm sorry I'm late," said Miles, his voice low and toneless.

"Mister Warren," Natalie stuttered breathlessly. "You need…You need to go back to the hospital-"

"I don't. I'm fine."

"But your…your face—"

"Go home Natalie."

Both parties turned to look at Pickman, whose voice cut through the room like a knife.

"I-"

"Go. Home."

Natalie lingered only half a moment longer, throwing a desperate look at Miles before fleeing away into the darkness. Pickman waited until the rhythmic clack of her footsteps faded from the stairway before continuing, during which time Miles didn't move a muscle. He hardly even blinked. When the echoing boom of the gallery's back door called from unseen darkness, Pickman took up his wine glass again.

"Take a seat, Mister Warren."

"No."

Pickman frowned, and halted mid-sip.

"You're not well."

"I told you, I'm fine. I've been lying down for days," Miles insisted, though his voice hardly rose at all. "They made me leave the apartment, Mister Pickman. I didn't want to."

"Listen to me now, Warren," Pickman said slowly and deliberately, "you're clearly in no state to work. Go back to the hospit—"

A shivering crash screeched through the office. In a single fluid movement Miles grabbed a paperweight from the edge of the desk and hurled it through the glass wall, sending fragments leaping to the floor in a waterfall of broken shards.

"I need to work!" Miles yelled, the first stab of any real emotion since he walked through the door. Such was the force of the shout that several sutures across his face burst, blood leaking in thin strings down his forehead and cheek. The two men stared at each other for a few moments, neither speaking. Then Miles shoulders dropped, his face blank.

"I need to work," he repeated, the renewed softness of his voice underscored by a steady *plit, plit, plit* of droplets hitting the floor. "I know what to do now, Mister Pickman. I've worked it out. Pinkest pink."

Pickman considered this for a moment, his wine glass now hovering frozen in mid-air. His eyes flicked from the puddles of broken glass to the little red streaks, before finally coming to rest on Miles' own. No longer hollow, he found. No, those eyes were filled with something he could not name. In the lull Miles leaned forward and laid his bloody palms flat against the desk.

"I've seen it," he insisted.

"Take me to the apartment, then. I shall see it for myself."

Miles' jaw tensed, and he shook his head.

"No. Not until it's ready. I'll take no more criticism from you, I *won't*. You try to see this before it's done Pickman and I swear I'll burn it all, I'll burn *everything*," he hissed. He was close enough now that Pickman could see his own distorted reflection in the glazed surface of his eyes, all warped and wrong. "I know what you were doing. I know you were pushing me, and pushing and *pushing* - but I understand it now. I forgive you. I wasn't where I needed to be for this to work but I am now. You have to let me show you."

"How can you be so sure?"

"Because you wouldn't have me in this gallery unless you believed I could make something truly beautiful. I can, now," Miles replied, voice suddenly descending into a pleading whisper. "Let me work, Pickman. Let me prove it."

Pickman swirled the notion around in his mouth, long seconds stretching into one another as he considered the scene before him. Then he set down the glass, and slowly steepled his fingers together.

"Do you have a sample?" he asked. Miles shook his head.

"No."

"Then what is any of this talk worth, Mister Warren?"

"It needs time. I can't bring it here, it's on the wall now. It has to be on the wall."

"And what am I supposed to do come July 18th? Remove the whole plaster section?"

"Yes. Take it out of my commission, I don't care," Miles replied flatly..

He hadn't blinked in over a minute now. "It'll be ready, Mister Pickman. I promise you it'll be ready; I know what to do now. I can see it."

Pickman stared into those glazed eyes long and hard. Still he could see nothing but the terrible passion, burning and boiling yet somehow cold as a freshly dug grave. A little part of him cried out to refuse. To run, and to end whatever this was before it truly began. But time had rendered that small part of him inert, beauty made it quiet, its keening voice muffled beneath geological layers of excess and experience.

"Then I believe you have work waiting for you," he said.

‡

The next two weeks were sleepless. Not for fear, or for shock, but for Pickman's curiosity. Every day and every night he thought on what Miles had said, what he had promised, and the possibilities danced like searchlights in a storm. He knew what he'd seen in Miles' eyes – or rather, knew he had seen *something*. Whatever emotions had stirred in the artist's gaze he could not name, a fact which only entangled him further in that deathly curiosity. He could not fathom it.

And yet, he told himself again and again, it was *real*. It was raw and rare, unnamed in the consciousness of the art world. A feeling only Miles Warren knew.

So, uncharacteristically, Pickman abided. No meetings, no visits, no contact – just the endless busywork and great vastness of the empty office, and the vaster void of the pale grey sky through the window. He waited, eroding like an old sea wall.

That was until the fifteenth day, when the tide finally won.

"What is it you want me to do, sir?" asked Oliver, the newest of the interchangeable faces. Natalie had never returned after that fateful night, and so the wheel turned. Pickman drew in a long, restrained breath through his nostrils.

"There is an artist in my care, a Miles Warren."

"Oh!" Oliver said, his blonde-framed face brightening. "The

man for the 18th."

"Don't interrupt me. His name is Miles Warren, he's in the apartments at Acacia Lane," Pickman said, casting a beady eye down to Oliver's empty hands. "Write this down."

Oliver fumbled out his smartphone, an act which made him look distinctly like a confused ape.

"20 Acacia Lane, apartment 13. He was recently in an accident, and I'd like you to take him some flowers."

"What kind of flowers?"

"*Any flowers.* Buy them down the street, it doesn't matter, just take them to him now."

A brief frown cracked Oliver's face, but it was nothing more than stupidity spasming his brow, Pickman decided.

"Yeah, I can get that done. I still have appointments to make."

"Listen to me now: the next part is very important. Once you're inside, I want you to find the art piece he's making for me. It should be on a wall, and the apartment is very small."

"Okay...?"

"Don't interfere with it," Pickman ordered sharply, narrowing his eyes. "Don't even touch it. Just look at it. Take it in, and once you've seen it I want you to return here *immediately*. Keep it fresh in your mind – but under *no circumstances tell him it's for me*, do you understand?"

Oliver blinked at him. The hesitancy didn't worry Pickman – one of the advantages of new blood was the overpowering desire to please.

"Okay, Mister Pickman. I'll do that," he replied after a few moments. Then he held up the phone. "I could take a picture if you want?"

"No, no pictures." Pickman sat back in his chair, shaking his head slowly like an opium dreamer. "Photographs are a stripped-down visual carcass; it wouldn't capture it. Use your memory." Oliver smiled amiably at him, and said something asinine before disappearing down the stairs.

Oliver smiled amiably at him, and said something asinine before disappearing down the stairs. Pickman had stopped listening the moment his needs were met, and now concentrated solely on that final wait. He sat in his chair unmoving, largely unblinking, existing only as a taut string resisting the urge to snap. Phones rang, but he ignored them. Messages sat unread. Ten minutes became an hour.

As noon arrived Pickman took up the office phone and punched in the assistant's number, but to no response. He tried again to the same effect, and again and again, breath becoming more hissed and frantic with each fruitless dial tone, rising like a fever pitch until another sound stopped him dead: a scream outside the window.

Pickman's chair clattered to the floor as he flung himself to his feet and rushed to the glass. A crowd gathered down in the square below, variously looking upwards and muttering to one another, the suspected screamer stood at the front with one hand clasped over her mouth. The other stood frozen in a horrified gesture, pointing towards the gallery.

No, Pickman realised. Not just the gallery, but the gallery *roof*.

He flew across the landing and down the stairway, tearing through crowds on the main floor. One man was knocked to the ground to the dismay of his companions but Pickman did not slow down, didn't even look back as he hurled himself out through the double doors and into the pale light of day. The crowd, now variously yelling, didn't even notice his sudden emergence. It was only as Pickman pivoted around that he found out why.

Oliver stood at the edge of the precipice, high enough that he was no more than a thin silhouette against the sky. Pickman went to call his name but found he didn't know it, and so instead let out a long, guttural sound. Oliver paid neither him nor the crowd any heed, tottering and swaying over the balustrade, the wind whipping his straw blonde hair into a woven death mask.

But beneath the wind and distance Pickman could make out brief flashes of Oliver's face, white as a sheet and frozen in slack-mouthed horror, and even more than that Pickman *swore* he could feel the boy's eyes upon him. Staring. Accusing.

Oliver lifted a foot over the edge. The crowd yelled and roiled, and threw up their hands as if to catch him, to push him back, but Pickman stayed still. Kept his eyes on the shape, listened. Oliver was shouting something up there, though from a distance it was utterly incomprehensible. Unable to contain himself any longer Pickman stepped forward and cupped his hands to his mouth, his own voice high with desperation as he yelled a question into the air.

A question doomed to remain unanswered.

In an instant, Oliver was gone. Just a shadow flitting down the face of the building, followed by the sound of a body hitting pavement. The crowd surged forward and knocked Pickman to the ground, the yelling now turning to screams - but it was only as the daze left him that Pickman realised the crowd had in fact gone deathly silent. They gathered around the unseen body like crows around carrion, utterly without sound save for muted whimpering.

The shouting was his own. Even as the corpse lay upon the ground, again and again Pickman repeated the only thing he had said since emerging from the gallery.

"What did you see!?" he shrieked. "*What did you see!?*"

‡

Beyond the car Pickman could see nothing. The canary-yellow glow of the internal lights cast sheets over the windshield and windows, blocking out everything but the suggestion of velvet darkness in every direction. By sight alone he could only be sure of the fact that night had fallen and little else, but that was better. Best not to see where he was going.

It had been six hours since the suicide. Four since the police left the gallery, and two since Pickman had parked the car. He watched hour by hour as the day ticked towards July 17th, the final day, bargaining back and forth with himself. But ultimately, even the short wait of twenty-four hours was too excruciating to bear.

Not that there was any doubt, of course. The dilemma was a false one, a frightened animal's brain fighting against the higher and more easily enraptured faculties of man. Despite his acute fear Pickman never doubted he would end up here. There was no doubt he would stay. And of course, ultimately, no doubt he would leave the safety of the vehicle's glow and venture into the outer darkness. He had passed the point where desire was the goal. Now it was prophecy.

He exhaled a stuttering cloud of smoke and went into the glove compartment, where two hastily stowed companions clattered against the plastic lid. The first was a gun, albeit not real – a metal replica, given to him by a director he didn't know in a celebration of a show he'd never seen. The second was a letter opener, real as real could be. He turned it in his hands, admiring the edge with more than a note of anxiety.

If all went wrong, he hoped, the gun's charisma would see him to safety. If not…

Pickman slipped the letter opener into his sleeve and shouldered his way out of the driver's seat. It didn't bear thinking about.

Acacia Lane sat on the south side of Mayfair, nestled secretively between neat townhouses and artisan coffee shops. By day its bricks gleamed proudly in the light, the meander of the serpentine road almost sensual in its curves. Wrought iron fences stood watch over polite little porches, the cold metal civilised by garlands of flowerbeds and potted trees.

But on moonless nights, when all was still and the viewer found themselves alone, Acacia Lane transformed. By the listless glow of streetlamps all sense of scale and distance disappeared. The winding streets seemed endless and fickle, twisting in all directions with no indication of exit. The wrought iron fences, cage-like, hosted shivering shapes that twitched in winds that were not there. The rows of townhouses, once petite, seemed to soar once they left the weak gleam of the light, as if the visible faces were no more than the roots of greater, more terrible structures. Structures that stretched in suggestion far up into the unseen blackness, primordial monuments to gods purposefully forgotten.

Pickman glanced up at them with wide eyes as he crept deeper down the lane. He felt watched, though he could not imagine by whom – or what. The car's headlights soon slid around a corner and disappeared, leaving him adrift in the labyrinth with only the dim outline of brass door numbers to guide him where his appetite demanded, but his heart feared to go. By the time number 20 loomed into view his grip on the stage pistol was white-knuckle, enough that he could feel the embossed 'fake' label on the handle pressing an imprint into his palm.

Yet still, unspeakable curiosity drove him on. Lifted his arm and with a shaking, almost unwilling hand, pressed the buzzer on his behalf. The button creaked in its housing, followed by the longest few seconds of quiet Pickman had ever known.

Until, a crackle. A dim hum from the speaker, indicating that another party – albeit silent themselves – had answered.

"Warren," he whispered into the intercom. "It's Pickman. Let me in."

No answer. But then, a loud *click* sounded from the lock, and the black front door jerked open. Pickman stayed frozen in front of it for a few seconds, his eyes on the brief gap between door and frame: a slit of tantalising darkness, so small and yet through which lay all the promised terrors and ecstasies he'd dreamt of. He held the gun close, and the hidden knife even closer. And then, Pickman entered.

The inside of number 20 was a black vault. Polished black bricks for walls, shining black tiles for floors, and anonymous rows of closed black doors leading to unknown rooms. At its centre lay a spiral staircase which Pickman mounted carefully, climbing until he finally arrived at the terminal landing: another long black hallway, at the end of which lay apartment 13.

Apartment 13, whose door lay open. Apartment 13, with no lights inside.

Pickman hovered at the edge of the stairway and compulsively shifted his grip on the stage gun.

"Warren," he called, his voice strained. "Are you there?"

No answer.

"Warren! Enough with these theatrics, come out!"

Silence. For a blind second Pickman felt his skin leap, every bone in his body aching to pull backwards and flee. But there in his chest, the gnawing; the ache. The need to know. Before he could stop himself Pickman took a step forward and plunged into the darkness.

The entrance hallway was a wreck. Even without light Pickman could make out misshapen piles of detritus climbing the walls, dark stains smeared over the floors and ceilings, and he groped blindly for a light switch only to find that none of them worked. Shivering, he produced the letter opener from his sleeve and clutched it close like a talisman, pressing further into the apartment, and further away from the light of the open door.

"Warren?" he whispered again. This time an answer, though not verbally: just after he spoke Pickman swore he heard a strange, dull shivering sound. Like a body convulsing against a wall, though he couldn't tell where. He gritted his teeth, easing open the living room door in the hopes of finding it empty. Then, he recoiled.

The smell was unlike anything Pickman had ever experienced. It was dizzying and thick, a corrosive fog of chemical fumes and organic odours, though nothing he could accurately identify. Had it been the iron tang of blood or the unmistakable nail-polish sting of turpentine he could have comprehended it, but this was all more abstract. Not bloody but *mineral,* as if the essence of bone marrow had been divorced from flesh and mixed with pure atoms of the artificial.

Pickman reeled back and vomited on the carpet, retching so violently that the letter opener fell from his hand. Supporting himself on the door frame he tried to get back up, but the fog was too dizzying to focus. Too thick to catch his breath. Through bleary vision he caught sight of murky shapes in the room beyond, incomprehensible piles and structures that now suggested purposeful construction.

And then, in his peripherals: movement.

"Pickman," croaked a voice. "I told you what would happen if you came here."

A shape rose from behind one of the structures, as if they'd been lying down on the floor. They were completely naked, pale flesh almost luminous in the gloom. Pickman's heart leapt into his throat as the shape drew closer but he found himself unable to move, rooted to the spot by fear and the disorientation of the gas.

"Don't come any closer," he stuttered, holding up the fake gun. The figure stopped just shy of the light, only its bare legs visible in the last of the front door's glow. They were covered in chemical sores.

"It's okay Mister Pickman," it cooed softly. "I won't burn it. I've done it. I want you to see."

With considerable effort Pickman raised his eyes, squinting into the dark. Miles' face was nothing more than a blur, a nothing, and yet somehow with a sense beyond sight Pickman could tell there was something wrong with it. Something only the animal part of his brain could recognize.

"What have you done?" he murmured. Miles raised an emaciated arm and pointed down the hall, and from somewhere inside the blur came the suggestion of an awful smile.

"Pinkest pink," it whispered. "Come and see."

The figure slipped away down another hallway, followed by the sound of a latch clicking open. All the time Pickman could hear Miles' voice becoming fainter and fainter, *come and see, come and see*, and with every exhortation Pickman felt the hunger in gnaw harder. The fear had sapped his will but the hunger only grew, the *need*. Sucking in a breath he stepped into the living room and followed the path of the pale shape around the corner, only to find it waiting only a few feet beyond.

Its hand lay on the doorknob.

"Are you ready?" it asked. Pickman didn't answer, and Miles let out a low, gurgling chuckle. Then, it opened the door.

‡

The 18th of July was a joyous affair. The Pickman Gallery, bathed in a heady summer sunlight, threw its doors wide to the great and the good. Packed into the main hall a group of dozens milled in expensive suits, tasteful hats, fake smiles, gliding from attraction to attraction like moths in the wind. Every so often a head would turn and conversation whirl towards the stage at the end of the room, and the large object sat upon it: a section of masonry, freshly dug from the walls of 20 Acacia Lane and covered in a jet-black sheet.

Pickman watched the proceedings with delight from the main stage, watching them go to and fro, back and forth. Ants, he thought. They all looked so much like ants.

Somewhere in the distance a clock struck midday, and Pickman tapped his glass. The sound rose above the din like a knife cutting through skin and all heads in the room turned as one towards him.

"Please take your seats, ladies and gentlemen," he called. "The main event is about to begin."

The crowd clumsily arranged themselves in their given places and the room became a sea of shiny spectacles and staring eyes, all of them trained on the stage. Yet still nobody seemed to notice Miles Warren, sat at his corner of the raised plinth, perfectly still. He wore a veil like a woman in mourning, the rest of him swaddled in the same pitch-black cloth as the wall, so that not even a patch of exposed flesh saw sunlight. Pickman turned to him regardless, smiling a wide, almost delirious smile. Even if he couldn't see it, he knew that Miles was smiling back.

"What is colour?" Pickman asked, prompting a muted wave of laughter from the audience. "A cliché, I know, but a question we are increasingly forced to contend with. Four months ago, with the release of Prime Blush, the public were asked to believe that art could be measured. Distilled. That true colour was nothing more than photons hitting the eye and that its essence could be manufactured in a lab, ready to be plastered on limited edition drinks and spray painted on a billionaire's car."

More laughter.

"But we know the truth, don't we? That in colour one finds not only the viewed, but the viewer. We know that colour is a frozen reflection, and without human flaws, human eyes, human *emptiness* to perceive it? In that case, there's no colour at all. When we plumb the depths of our human flaws to the very bedrock, even the simplest of hues can become transcendent. Perhaps even divine."

His fingers teased tightly around the edge of the black fabric.

"I'm pleased to present our central piece, *A Moment's Excess* by Miles Warren," he announced, "Or as I've taken to calling it: Pinkest Pink."

The veil came away. Someone at the back of the room screamed.

Within seconds the entire crowd were screaming with them, throwing over their chairs in a panic, running to the side of the room to hammer at the locked doors. Some clawed at their own faces. Others keeled over. But Pickman saw none of it: he could only stare at his creation through tears of joy.

It was beautiful.

It was so, so beautiful.

Jacob Close is a career writer from Scotland with a cool face and handsome opinions. He's been everything from a theatre critic and magazine editor to a lowly corporate copywriter, but has since decided that going insane as a freelance novelist was the better option. His first book series, "The Branch" can be bought at all major bookstores and is published with Vulpine Press."

Polyptych of an Invisible Boy

Kyle Tam

Adrian

How long would you last if you were invisible? I've been transparent as long as I can remember. Do you know what it's like? To be ignored by those around you? You get jostled and pushed around, not because you're in the way, but because you're just not there. The people around me don't know it, but they're invisible too. But I know it. I'm the only one who sees.

Everybody thinks they're special, but they're wrong. We're all identical drops in the same ocean. Lonely, drifting, and not one of us unique.

Me? I'm the plainest of all.

I was born to an average suburban family. My dad worked as a middle manager, filing papers for deals he hadn't brokered, and making phone calls to people who didn't matter.

My mom was a housewife in the most literal sense, spending all of her time at home. I love my parents, but they don't really get me. And it doesn't seem like there's anything to "get" about them. As for me… well, besides my crooked nose, I think I look alright. Not a movie star, but not hideous either. Just… fine.

As a kid I wasn't bullied. Being bullied means you've managed to get people to give a shit. I'd see kids shoved in lockers or given wedgies and think, "God, I wish that were me". Nobody came up to me or asked me to play. Nobody would pass me crayons. Nobody cared. Life became a cycle of simply existing. I was a mindless thing with no passion and no purpose.

Until I met her.

Mrs. Russell

She came to us halfway through the school year, father gripping onto her shoulders and mother giving me a vacant half-smile. I didn't ask questions, and they didn't provide answers.

We welcomed her with open arms, just like any other student, and she was placed into my homeroom.

Her assigned "buddy", as we like to call them, was one of my less cooperative children. Not a troublemaker by any means, just more solitary than I would have liked. When she entered the room, I saw that sullen boy sit up and take notice for the very first time. It was just enough for me to realise what an opportunity this was. Just enough to pull the trigger.

For the first time, I saw him smiling in class. Not smirking but actually smiling. Finally, progress! They became fast friends, and I'd often catch him whispering to her in class or passing her notes. Of course, I never called it out. Who am I to get in the way of young love? That being said, time passes and circumstances change. She was always surrounded by people to chat and laugh with, while he was relegated to the corner. Shrinking into himself. A fly on the wall.

It's not hard to understand why he brought that knife to school.

Jake

It was World History. Third period. I wasn't paying attention, talking to my friend Mitchell. He walked in wearing a ratty grey hoodie, trying to be invisible again. Poor dude. I remember looking at his hands and going silent. All of us did. You see it in the news, about some idiot with a knife or a gun holding schools hostage. You never think it'll happen to you.

He was shaking like crazy when he held that knife up. I don't think he was serious about it, really. Just upset and not thinking clearly. Called her out with his voice all hoarse, told her to come up to the front. I keep thinking about it, at night when I should be sleeping. Thinking about whether we should've stepped in, taken the knife out of his hands. Maybe things would've been different. But we were all frozen. Paralysed.

So she walks there slowly. Real slowly. He's saying how much he likes her and how much she means to him and it's not fair that she keeps ignoring him. We're all quiet, but I know everyone's thinking the same thing. About him. About her. Nothing… bad, but nothing good either. Just the kind of thing that makes you look at those teary eyes and understand where they're coming from. We've all been in that place, right? The one that leaves you staring at the ceiling, wondering where things went wrong. I thought, okay, this is gonna be a "come to Jesus" moment and they're gonna cry it out and it'll be okay.

Then she took that knife and stabbed him.

Carrie

People say I asked for this to happen. I didn't. I didn't ask my dad to have a mid-life crisis and move us to the middle of nowhere. I didn't ask my teacher to assign me a school guide
that I had to be nice to and ask questions like a good girl. I didn't ask my

classmates to spread rumours about how close we were, and keep making jokes about us. I didn't ask him to try and get close to me. All I asked for was the time of day and where the cafeteria was.

I never wanted to be perfect. I wanted to be normal, but now I can't even be that. I mess up one time and- No, I didn't even mess up. I was trying to defend myself. The cops know it, the law knows it, and God definitely knows it. Only the people around me don't. Now I'm a violent freak, and they worship the ground he walks on. Really? I'm not stupid or blind, you know. I saw the way people bypassed him in the halls, moving to the side wherever he walked. I saw them sit away from him during lunch, or share worried looks and whispers whenever he approached. I heard him rant about them, too, how everyone was some entitled this or degenerate that. But now that he's got a sob story, everyone's pretending that they're buying his poor tortured soul act?

The nerve of some people.

Kyle Tam is a dreamer, writer, and full-time complainer from the Philippines. Her fiction has been published in Idle Ink, Mineral Lit, and Analogies & Allegories among others. She also creates tabletop games, including the IGDN Honorable Mention MORIAH. You can find her on X and Blusky at @PercyPropa, or find her work at whatkylewrites. carrd.co.

The Book of I

Brian Gatti

RE: Request - Case Review

Thomas ███████

May 11, 2019

David,

I got your message about the case of Amelia
Bronwyn, 27F. It took some time to compile it
all.
You were right, this needs further action on
our part.
Let me know what you want me to do.

Sincerely,

Thomas
Field Director — North American Ops

Enclosed are scans of:
Journal (2/2/19 - 3/30/19)
Grosse Pointe Tribune Clipping (4/7/19)
Police report (4/4/19) (excerpts)
Hospital records (3/9/19 & 3/12/19) (excerpts)
TH Case summary & recommendations 5/11/19)

CC:
KM, Records
JT, Enforcement

February 9, 2019

    I have never been much for journaling, but my doctor thinks it would be a good idea for me to do it. She said by writing my experiences down, I can keep a grasp on objective reality.

    Whatever that means.

    I am the head of early childhood development at Grosse Pointe Academy. I always wanted to work with young kids. I have two loving parents who are traveling the world on a well-earned retirement vacation.

    Life was simple. Dating. Working. Small local trips. Not exactly Sex and the City, but it was good for me.

    Then everything went to hell.

    I remember it starting with the Book of Letters series. I was at the library looking for inspiration for class content when one of the librarians recommended them.

    Kids books written for the 3 to 6 age range. Each book takes a letter and wraps a story around it, using each letter in a sentence.

    There are millions of books out there like it.

    I found a complete set on eBay for $20, which might not sound like a big deal, but it's impossible to find. All the sets I'd seen were missing the Book of I.

It was just a Tuesday afternoon. Nothing special.

When they came, they were great. Each was colorful and well cared for. Vintage-looking, the series was published in the early 20s. The art was sort of abstract, but the images were friendly and appealing.

I didn't realize something was weird until I set them all up on my office shelf. Sitting in the 9th spot was the Book of I. Unlike the others, the colors were faded, and the spine's lettering was skewed as though misprinted. It stood out like an infected tooth in a mouth full of white teeth.

Just writing this is giving me anxiety. I need a break. Did I remember to turn the stove off? Shit. I should check.

February 13, 2019

Sorry for taking so long to come back to this. Dr. Ni told me I needed to get back to this to help me.

I met Dr. Wojian Ni when my parents made me get help with everything going on. I didn't want to, but they wanted me to see someone who could help me process everything going on. She insists I need to stay focused on my treatment, and writing down what happened is important.

The kids were enjoying the book of letters materials, and I was able to create all kinds of activities, I started making puppets based on the characters. It was cute and harmless. Right?

I felt an odd sense of revulsion when I opened the Book of I. It's the best way to describe it, like a visceral sense of something disgusting, but it felt so irrational I disregarded it.

I wish I hadn't.

Like all the books, the first page introduced us to the character. This one was Izzy. Usually, the characters were normal kids with a surprising diversity, considering the age of the publication.

But Izzy was different. She had a pale face with black scribbles for eyes and a mouth. Her hair was a chaotic swirl of black that wrapped around her body.

The next page showed Izzy in front of a house with the words, 'I see you.' It creeped me out.

I have to stop now and run some errands. Need to get gas for the car, I should get it checked, it must have a leak.

February 14, 2019

Every time I think of the book, I feel like Izzy is getting closer to me. I told Dr. Ni it's like she's staring at me everywhere I go.

I first confessed my feelings about it to my best friend Ti, she's the 3rd grade art teacher at the school. The kids call her Ms. Vedo. She was a good friend, but she didn't take me seriously. I wouldn't.

I tried to stop thinking about it but kept seeing her face.

I looked in the mirror for the first time today in weeks. She was there, a drawing on the wall behind me. Watching me. Seeing me. When I turned around, there was nothing.

I don't even know where the book is anymore. I wish she'd leave me alone.

I need to focus. Hold on, there's someone at the door. It must be the guy from the gas company, I've been smelling something weird in the house.

Ok, back. No one was there, probably just neighborhood kids.

The rest of the book is so strange. Despite my feeling of fear, I went back to it. Compelled.

Page 3 has Izzy in front of the same house but closer.

You could see a window in the front with Izzy saying 'I see you.'

Page 4 shows a woman in the window reading a book. Izzy is looking in the window with the words, I see you above the illustration.

Did you know the book was published on September 3rd, 1921? The illustrator was not the same as the other books. The only one with a different artist, Yatebya Vizhu.

I looked her up. Yatebya was an immigrant who fled the Russian Revolution. Unsurprisingly, there was little detail about her life, just that her art made her a target of those in power. She committed suicide shortly after the book was published.

I wasn't surprised when I read that, and I'm still not sure why.

Even being in the hospital is no escape for me.

We had an ice storm a few weeks ago.

The roads were icy. You need to be careful with Michigan roads when it's bad, but I was distracted. I thought I saw her black scribble eyes in my rear-view mirror, watching me.

I was only distracted for a moment, but it was enough. I took the turn too fast and spun out, hitting a tree.
I woke up in the ICU.

The doctor said I was lucky. I'd been unconscious for a week. They couldn't reach my parents, who were out of contact on vacation on the island of 'Arak; my only other emergency contact was Dr. Ni.
My life is pathetic.

Dr. Ni brought me my journal, so here I am writing.

Page 5 of the book showed the woman clearly. I thought she kind of looked like me. Izzy was at the door saying, as always, I see you.

This is getting to me. Ok, push through.

Dr. Ni said my thoughts of the woman looking like me are understandable —

we unconsciously frame the unfamiliar with familiar contexts.

I think she's full of shit, but what do I know? I'm the crazy one.

Page 6 showed the inside of the house with Izzy next to the woman. I have a mole on my right cheek. The woman did, too. Dr Ni said I'm looking for validation of my delusions. I think it's me. As always, Izzy says I see you.

Last night, I saw Izzy in my dreams. She was screaming without sound, staring at me with her scribble eyes.

Page 7 showed me getting ready for bed. The woman, not me. Not me. Right? Of course not me. And Izzy was in the bed waiting. I see you.

March 21, 2019

Yesterday was a pretty terrible fucking day.

The day started simply enough. I'd been back to school for about a week. The kids were so sweet and supportive. I dropped the whole letter books and switched to some materials I'd done earlier in the school year. I'd been feeling kind of normal, and the meds Dr. Ni put me on seemed to be helping. I hadn't seen Izzy in that time.

Two nights ago, I lost my new meds. They just went missing. I called Ni for more, but she was out of the office. I had to go without.

So yesterday. Let's talk about yesterday.

I freaked out. I was doing a storybook with my kids when I saw Izzy sitting in the circle with them. Her hair stretched out to cover the kids, revealing her naked body. It was covered in scratches and cuts. She looked like someone had thrown the drawing through a window.

None of the kids saw her, but I did. Taunting me. Seeing me. I started screaming. The kids were terrified. The police were called. No charges were filed, but I was fired.

Thankfully, Dr. Ni agreed to keep helping me without insurance.

Ti helped me pay for some things so I didn't lose my house, but I could tell she was done with me and my crazy.

Dr Ni was able to help me get a hold of my parents, as they were in a place where they could be contacted. I didn't speak to them directly; I was sedated for a while, but he explained everything. They sent me money, and I could pay Dr. Ni my bills and repay Ti for all the cash she'd been lending me since my accident.
I used the new payment app, Teveo, to pay her back, but it was the last time she spoke to me. I miss her.

It's cold in here. The heat isn't working. Did I pay the gas bill?

Ok. Pushing through. Almost done, I think.

Page 8 showed the woman in a car, driving with Izzy in the back. It was an old-style car, a black model T, but it was snowy out, and Izzy's scribble eyes were in the mirror. The page said I see you. Of course you do, you psycho bitch.

Fuck Izzy. Fuck her to hell. Fuck!!!

The goddamn book predicted my accident. Dr. Ni said it was a coincidence. I wish I could find the book to show her, to prove it.

Page 9 showed the hospital with me lying in bed.

Instead of tubes and wires attached to the woman, it was Izzy's hair. Invading her body. Invading MY body. I see you.

It makes my skin crawl. I can feel her hair in my brain. Her scribble eyes were staring at me.

March 21, still

Oh, what hell I'm in.

Dr. Ni said my parents called her. They're worried about me and having travel issues trying to get home; apparently, their plane had some kind of fuel leak. She gave them an update about me, that I'm getting better. I'm not, but she said it was the right thing to do.
Why worry them needlessly?
We even recorded a video of me to send to them.

Dr. Ni is pushing me to finish recording my experiences. I just want to be done. She said I almost am and it'll be so freeing to put it all down on paper. I'll be able to get my life back.
I hope so.

I'd like to see the kids again. I know I can't. The academy was very clear. I'm never to return. I miss the kids.

They were my family.

I know it's pathetic. So what, I loved them.

I'm so lonely. It's just me and Dr. Ni and my imaginary tormentor.

I tried calling Ti to say sorry and explain, but her line was disconnected. Just the dead robot voice, 'your call cannot be completely as dialed, error code 9321.'

I get it. I'd abandon me, too.

Page 9 showed the woman sitting in a chair with Izzy behind her, Izzy's hair wrapped around the woman's face. Smothering her. It must've been hard to breathe. And, of course, the words, I see you.

I see you. I see you. I see you!!

Ik zie je. Anata ga mietemasu.

I wish I could find the book. I don't know where it went. It's not in my box of stuff from the school. I'd fucking burn it and laugh.

I hope Yatebya Vizhu is in hell for drawing that soulless bitch.

Dr. Ni says this aggression I'm feeling is a manifestation of my feelings of unworthiness and self-loathing. I miss my parents. I wish they weren't gone. It's been so long. Why did they have to leave?

Sometimes, I feel it's my fault they left, but that's ridiculous.

I take pills to sleep. Sometimes, it keeps me from seeing Izzy and her eyes. It keeps her from seeing me. Those nights of emptiness are the best. Just peace.

Underneath it all, I can't say I'm surprised.

Dr. Ni got a call. My parents' flight back is delayed again. They're never coming home, I think.

Their disappointment in me is too much, I think. What else could it be?

I'm 27 with no job, husband, or kids. I'm just their crazy daughter. Thankfully, they are still helping me financially, but it's not enough. I think the power is off at my house. The nights are so cold, but I have a fireplace that helps. I've had to take to burning some furniture to keep warm.

Dr. Ni says that I'm okay this way. I shouldn't be scared.

I don't think I am scared anymore.

I remembered the last page of the book last night. It was a weird sort of dream. Izzy was there along with Dr. Ni, Ti, and my parents. Her hair was wrapped around everyone, and there was a place in the middle for me.

Strangely, it didn't feel lonely anymore. It felt more like being with those who loved me.

I woke up crying.

Page 10 showed a woman in an empty, broken-looking house. The woman looked as broken and filthy as the home. Izzy stood nearby with her hair twisted into the letter O.

'I see you,' said the page.

I see you too, Izzy.

I'm going to call Dr. Ni today and let her know I've figured it out. I'm better now.

I see you.

Woman found dead in family home

Amelia Bronwyn was found dead of apparent suicide in the abandoned home of her parents, Stephen and Linda Bronwyn.

Grosse Pointe PD conducted a routine well visit to the reclusive woman. A lack of response at the door prompted the officers to enter, and her body was discovered.

Stephen and Linda died on September 3rd, 2018, when a gas leak from the stove asphyxiated them. Their daughter, Amelia, lived in the home and worked as a teacher at Grosse Pointe Academy until parent complaints resulted in her termination.

Amelia moved into her parent's home shortly after their deaths, sustained by a small inheritance left to her by her parents.

People who knew her remarked that Amelia became withdrawn and increasingly paranoid after her parents died. She was briefly hospitalized for an accident but left before discharge.

Services will be held at Grosse Pointe Methodist Church, and donations are requested to the American Society for Suicide Prevention.

Police Department Report

Case No: ___019-0004-5456-9409___   Date: _4/4/2019_

Officer: _____Jacobs and Villay_____

Incident/issue: ___Routine wellness check___

Description of event/issue:

0903:
Knocked at the door three times. Jacobs walked the exterior of the home. No broken windows. No signs of activity. Mail piled in the mailbox.
Knocked on the side dining window and back door. No response.
Called dispatch and received permission to use the vacation key.

0907:
Opened rear door to the kitchen. House was dark and a strong stench came out.
Garbage was scattered on the floor. It appeared as though the room had been intentionally damaged. We called out and received no response.
Moved to dining room. More trash. House was very cold. Likely heat had not been on for a while.
Creepy drawings on the wall of people with scribbled-out eyes and mouths.
Above the drawings was written in large letters, I see you.

[Black and white photo included - The dining room is cramped with trash. A fireplace is visible in the living room to the right. The drawings cover the walls, looking as though a child did them. A large decorative mirror on the wall has been shattered.]

0910:
Upstairs we found Amelia hanging from a ceiling beam. The rope was strange, maybe nylon? Looked like thickly braided hair.
She was dead. She looked thin and her pale body was covered in cuts and scrapes.

[Black and white photo included - Amelia's body hanging limply from the hairlike rope. Her naked skin is visible through her long hair, pale flesh torn as though by broken glass. Wounds showed signs of infection.]

Gross Point County Hospital
Inpatient Visit Summary

Name: Doe, Isabelle   Gender: F   DOB:

Race: White (Caucasian)   Ethnicity: Not Hispanic or Latino

Primary Language: English   PCP:

Visit Information:

Reason(s) for visit:

Automotive accident

Brain injury

Lacerations to face and arms

Malnutrition

Exhibit D -
Hospital records
3/9/19 & 3/12/19
(excerpts)

Attending notes:

Patient was admitted after an accident. She was unconscious and there was no identification with her. A note in her pocket seemed to indicate she is under the care of a psychiatrist, Dr. Wojian Ni. We were unable to find anyone with this name licensed to practice medicine in Michigan.

Examination of the patient revealed trauma to the head and superficial cuts on her face and arms due to the accident.

Patient appeared to be undernourished, and her body was covered in wounds, many of which were old and poorly healed.

Recommend psychiatric evaluation for DTS and possible commitment to long-term care.

Patient says her name is Isabelle.

Gross Point County Hospital
Inpatient Discharge Summary

Name: Doe, Isabelle   Gender: F   DOB:

Primary Language: English   PCP:

Date of admittance: 3/9/2019   Date of discharge: 3/12/2019

Discharge Information:

Reason(s) for visit:

Automotive accident
Brain injury
Lacerations to face and arms
Malnutrition

Attending notes:

Patient left hospital 3/12/2019 AMA and without release. Police
were called and a description was provided.

Exhibit E: TH Summary

1. Amelia was wracked with guilt over her parents' deaths, and the grief became unmanageable.
2. Amelia was terminated well before the date in her journal. The head of the school cited her erratic and troubling behavior.
3. Amelia acquired a legitimate copy of the Book of I. This means prior elimination efforts were ineffective, or the Book can reform (eBay seller username is IcyEwe9321 - only one sale, likely a dead end).

We should raise the priority on this item as our attempts at destroying it were ineffective.

While the risk for mass impact is low, the insidious nature of the artifact and its apparent ability to recreate itself means there is a risk of escalation.

The next step is to investigate the original publishing house and find the source of the Book.

Sincerely,

Thomas ███████

Brian Gatti lives in Phoenix, Arizona with his wife, son, daughter, a long-suffering dog, and two bossy guinea pigs. He has been working on his writing for the last 33 years, sidetracked by many things but always hearing the voices of my characters, begging for their stories to be told. He has been a full time writer since the summer of 2023.

BEARING SERPENTS

C.W. Blackwell

The county jail sent me home in the same blood-stained clothes they'd booked me in. Dead phone, seven dollars in my wallet. I didn't live far, just a few short blocks up Ocean Street in a scabby little studio above an all-night diner. I'd only been jammed up for a few days, but they'd already changed the locks and posted an eviction notice to the front door. Sure, I owed plenty of back-rent. But there's some irony in waiting three months to get the garbage disposal fixed, only to have the locksmith install a new deadbolt in less time than it takes to say *criminal malfeasance.*

I sat on the stairwell, watching the street with my head in my hands. Nowhere to go, all my bridges burned. The fog had rolled in and the streetlights bled orange in the haze. It was three, maybe four o'clock in the morning. I opened my wallet and counted the ones, tipped a few dimes into my palm. It wasn't much, but depending on who was working the night shift at the diner, I could get a full breakfast and maybe a cup of coffee on the sly.

The diner was empty, some late-seventies balladeer crooning from the overhead speakers. I could hear the cooks in the back, joking and laughing. I took a seat at the counter and drummed the silverware on my thighs. I wasn't in any hurry. After a few minutes, a tall brunette came out from the back with a smile that quickly faded when she saw me.

"Sorry to ruin your night," I said.

"Honey, my night was bound to get ruined one way or another." She looked me over and pressed a pen to the order pad. "Know what you want?"

"How much is your free coffee?"

I winked when I said it, but she didn't catch on.

"We don't sell free coffee here," she said. "Just the payin' kind."

"Sandy working tonight?"

"Sandy don't work here no more."

"What happened to her?"

"Got fired for givin' out free coffee."

"Well then, I'll take the lumberjack breakfast. Eggs over-medium."

"Anything to drink?"

"Water."

The order came quickly, and it was everything I'd hoped for. The kitchen sink of breakfasts. The whole damn boat. I was elbows-deep in pancakes and bacon when a man slipped onto the stool beside me. I eyed him while I chewed. Mid-thirties, clean cut. Decent-looking guy. He smiled broadly, but it seemed off, like he was having an amusing conversation with himself. I glanced around the diner at all the other places he could have sat.

"You got blood on your shirt," he said. "You have an accident?"

I finished chewing, not in any hurry to answer.

"That's what they tell me," I said. "You some kind of private investigator?"

"No," he said, laughing. "Not a private investigator."

"Well, look man. I'm not looking to make a new friend."

He laughed again. I was having a hard time figuring out what was so damn funny. I was about to politely tell him to fuck off when he said: "I came in here hoping to buy you a cup of coffee."

His name was Lucas, and the tale he told was a strange one. Lucky for him, I really needed the coffee. He said one of the COs at the jail tipped him off when they saw my tattoos at intake. I had plenty of tattoos, but the one that interested him was the pair of rattlesnakes inked around my left forearm. I rolled up my sleeve and showed him. He admired the tattoos for a moment, then rolled up his sleeve and showed his own.

"So you run some kind of snake tattoo club?" I said.

"It's so much more than that. We're ophiophilists."

"You'll have to translate that for me."

"We love snakes. Their histories, mythologies."

"I bet you do. But lots of people get snake tattoos."

"Yes, they do." That laugh again. "But your name came up at the right time. See, we're always looking for signs and portents. And we love to give a helping hand."

"Buddy, I need more than a cup of coffee."

"We all do," he said. "If only life were that simple, right?" He unpocketed a Bic pen from his jacket pocket and wrote an address on a paper napkin. "That's why we'd like you to visit our little spot in the mountains."

I glanced at the napkin.

"Boulder Creek?"

"Yes. We're up an old dirt road just before the State Park."

"I try to avoid the mountains."

"I try to avoid the city, yet here I am."

Lucas told me all I had to do was agree to visit and he'd not only pay for my breakfast, but he promised to give me whatever he was holding in his hand as well. He sat there, that goofy grin ear to ear, with his fist aloft. The waitress had disappeared, and I couldn't hear the cooks goofing around anymore. There weren't even any cars on the road, just traffic lights cycling through the empty streets.

"I'm too old for that game," I said. "And so are you."

"It's no game," said Lucas. "We'd like to get you back on your feet again."

Any other night I might have walked, maybe even knocked him off his stool. I'd seen all sorts of scams, ran a few grifts myself. But I was also damn curious what was in his hand. Money? Jewelry? A tiny snake?

"Fine," I said, stuffing the napkin in my pocket. "I'll come. Now it's your turn."

He opened his hand.

A house key—brand new and freshly-cut.

"I said I'd visit, not move in, man."

"It's not a key to my door."

"Then what is it?"

"It's a key to your door."

‡

When I went upstairs, the eviction notice had been removed. I stood at the door with the shiny brass key in my hand, taking a quick glance around to check if some camera crew would come running up to reveal the prank. I slid the key in and twisted the lock.

First thing I noticed was the place looked pretty clean. Much cleaner than I'd left it. The carpets had been vacuumed, kitchen mopped. On the coffee table was a stack of new clothes. Jeans, t-shirts, underwear. A fresh box of tennis shoes the same size and brand as the ones I was wearing. Even the refrigerator had been cleaned out and restocked with food. There was a snake magnet pinning down a photograph to the freezer door, a group of people sitting beneath a large redwood tree, smiling and waving to the camera. Some had long, fat snakes draped over their shoulders.

SEE YOU SOON, STEVE, it said in black sharpie.

"See you soon, weirdos," I said to the photo.

I drank whatever booze I could find in the cupboards and went to bed, thinking of all the different places I would have slept if I hadn't been able to get into my apartment again: the park, the east side shelter, the Arco station bathroom. As weird as the snake freaks were, I couldn't help but think fondly of them while I drifted off to a hard and dreamless sleep. Still, something bothered me: they couldn't have cleaned and stocked the apartment in the time it took to eat my breakfast downstairs. They'd planned it longer than Lucas was letting on, and that meant I needed to be careful.

I woke mid-afternoon and headed down the street, cycling through all my missed voicemails. I'd walked all the way to Water Street before I heard my boss's message giving me the can. Lucky for him, I was standing right in front of the shop when I heard it. I went straight through the shop bay doors and found him rifling through my toolbox.

"Now I know where all my tools are going," I said.

He hadn't seen me walk in, and I startled him. He turned with a filter wrench in one hand and a bologna sandwich in the other, eyes like moons.

"Steve," he said. "I didn't think you'd get out so soon."

"It's expensive keeping non-violent offenders in the clink."

"Well, I'm sorry." He set the wrench on the tool tray and bit a corner off his sandwich. "But that little stunt you pulled made the news big time. I can't have you wrenching here no more."

"Nobody got hurt, Al."

"You're lucky nobody got hurt. They say you ran three cars off the road before landing in the cereal aisle of that 7-Eleven on Laurel Street. I saw the security footage of that last bit on YouTube. The whole world saw it by now, I'm sure. I take it you're on probation or something?"

"They call it supervised release."

"I'm surprised they let you out at all."

"It's funny, but I don't remember a thing."

He looked me up and down—I could tell he was curious about my new clothes.

"Listen, man," he said. "I'll keep your tools safe till the end of the month. After that, I can't guarantee anything. You know how stuff wanders off."

I asked if he had a final check, and he told me to follow him to the office where he printed one out and gave a clammy handshake.

"One more thing," he said, as I turned to leave. "Where'd you get those clothes?"

"I made some new friends, Al."

"Jail friends?"

"No, snake friends."

"Sounded like you said snake friends just now."

I snatched the bologna sandwich, took a bite, and handed it back to him. "I did say snake friends, Al. And if you know what's good for you, you'd cut back on the mayo."

‡

By the time I cashed my check, picked up a fresh bottle of bourbon at The Grog Shop, and ate another lumberjack breakfast, it was almost sundown. Commuters had returned, clogging the intersections on Ocean Street as streetlights brightened down the avenue. I had just started up the stairwell to my apartment when a voice called to me.

"Shoes fit, buddy?"

It was Lucas. He sat on the hood of a newer model Subaru with his arms folded and that big weird grin spreading wide.

"A little tight, but they'll break in," I said.

"I'm sure they will. Wanna go for a ride?"

"To Boulder Creek?"

"You guessed it." He spun the car keys on his finger, smiling up at me. "The others want to meet you. I told them I'd drop by and pick you up."

"I'm not up for it," I said. "I lost my job today. I was going to drown my sorrows."

"We've got plenty of booze—and no sorrows at all."

I glanced up at the apartment, shook my head.

"I should really start looking for a job," I said.

"Don't worry about rent. You're paid up through the end of next month. We all made sure of it."

"No shit?"

"You're one of us now. We take care of each other."

"It's not a sex thing, is it?"

"No, not a sex thing."

Every nerve seemed to be pulling me back up the stairwell toward the bottle of bourbon. I wanted to get sauced, not sing "Kumbaya" with Lucas. Still, the new clothes were real, and so was the front door key in my pocket. So far, they'd made good on their promises, and a part of me wanted to milk it as far as it would go.

"You said you got booze?" I said.

Lucas gave a slow, serious nod.

"We got plenty, man. Wine, whiskey, whatever. Real good shit."

"How good?"

"Real good."

He was starting to speak my language.

‡

We took River Street to HWY 9, past old trailer parks rotting along the river, past the town of Felton with its all-night laundromats and Pentecostal churches. It was dark now. Redwoods crowded the highway so you couldn't see the moon or stars. Just the night bugs zipping through the headlights and a broken yellow line that reeled on toward Boulder Creek.

We passed the town's main drag, and it wasn't long before Lucas pulled off the road and eased the Subaru up a narrow rock driveway that led deep into the Santa Cruz Mountains. He kept looking over at me and smiling, but it wasn't easing my nerves at all. I imagined those teeth growing longer somehow, sharper. A part of me wanted to jump out and hightail back to the city, but another part—the broke part—wanted to let it ride.

The driveway ended in a circle around an old-growth redwood tree, and there were lighted cabins just visible through the tanoak scrub. Much further back, I could see a large Victorian house through the trees. Lucas parked along the driveway, and already folks began filtering out from the cabins to meet me. They seemed nice enough—maybe a little too nice—and everyone knew my name. We compared snake tattoos, and soon the group was ushering me toward the Victorian house where a large bonfire brightened the front yard.

A tall brunette wandered over with a boa constrictor draping her shoulders and a bottle of Bulleit bourbon in her hands, the same kind I'd bought just a few hours ago at the Grog Shop. She poured a glass and handed it to me, told me her name was Sheila. Along her index fingers were tiny rattlesnake tattoos with the rattles curling up on her knuckles.

"You know my brand," I said, although I wasn't really that surprised

"There's a whole case in the guest house," said Sheila. "Don't be shy."

I knocked the glass back and she poured another. Everyone was standing around the bonfire as if waiting for something to happen. Nine, maybe ten people total. The fire, the snakes, the booze—so far it was all pretty much what I'd expected.

"Lucas must be pretty wealthy to make all this work," I said.

Sheila laughed, and the snake's head bobbed on her shoulders.

"If you think Lucas runs this place, you'd better think again."

"Who runs the place?"

"We don't really believe in hierarchy, here. Snakes don't either. But I'd be lying if I said Vienna wasn't in charge. She runs the main house and most of the finances. She also gets first dibs on newcomers like you."

I swallowed hard.

"What do you mean first dibs?"

"In bed, of course. She's a very talented lover."

"She sleeps with everyone who joins? I thought this wasn't a sex thing."

"Well, it's not. But Vienna is polyamorous. We all are."

"Are snakes polyamorous?"

"Of course they are. You didn't know?"

A man appeared with an armload of firewood and dumped it into the fire, and as the fire grew hotter, others wandered through the smoke with offerings of their own. I met a woman named Glenda from the East Bay, who gave up a tech job in Silicon Valley to join the group. She brought a freshly baked bread roll with a tub of hand-churned butter. Another was a nonbinary librarian named Blaise who brought a plate of assorted cheeses. There was a plumber from Los Angeles. A dentist from

Venezuela. All seemed to have joined not through some internet outreach or listserv, but through a network of group members who actively recruited them. All had multiple snake tattoos, and several had surgically forked their tongues.

"Attention, everyone."

A voice came from somewhere above the fire, and it took me a moment to find the speaker. A woman stood behind a white balustrade on the second floor of the Victorian. Long red hair down to her waist, skin glowing in the moonlight. She looked like a movie star from some bygone era, and she wore an enormous python around her neck like jewelry. Maybe there were two pythons. "Please raise your glasses to Steve Harris from Santa Cruz, our newest friend and honorary member. May his worries be our worries, may our strength be his strength."

Everyone toasted and cheered.

"Was that Vienna?" I asked Blaise. They were sipping from a glass of red wine, watching the woman recede from the balustrade.

"Yes," they said. "Isn't she lovely?"

"She's got dibs on me, you know?" I said it as a joke, but I realized part of me wished it were true. The way Vienna stood over the group with her beautiful red hair and classic Hollywood charm was so strangely alluring.

Blaise gave a knowing smile and finished the wine in their glass.

"It's an honor to be chosen," they said. "It would be a night you'd never forget."

‡

The fire cooled and the bourbon did me in. Lucas walked me down a lighted path that led to the guest house, a Spanish-style bungalow with adobe walls and a terracotta roof. Something you'd more likely see overlooking the ocean than deep in a redwood forest. Inside was clean and well-kept. Fresh linens on the bed, a vase of white lilies on the kitchen counter. Lucas motioned to the coffee table where a stack of clothes lay with a handwritten note.

"It's from Vienna," he said.

"What does it say? I'm too drunk to read cursive."

"It says to change into these clothes and meet her in the main house at eleven-thirty."

I glanced at my phone: 10:45. "What's wrong with the clothes I'm wearing?"

"She has a particular way of doing things," said Lucas. "Why don't you take a shower? I'll make a pot of coffee to clear the cobwebs."

By the time I'd showered, changed, and sucked down half a cup of coffee, it was almost time to meet Vienna. Lucas held me by the elbow as we wound through the dark redwood groves toward the Victorian house below. I could still smell the bonfire smoldering and there was now a slight fog hanging in the trees. Lucas brought me to the front door and gently knocked, the soft flicker of candlelight playing in the windows.

Vienna answered in a flowing white robe with black and yellow snakes embroidered down the sleeves. It looked like less of a lounge piece and more ceremonial in nature. Her eyes were so green I could even make them out in the candlelight. She was a few inches taller than me, and the way she stood with her arms loosely folded against the cold made her look so poised and confident.

"Hello Steven," she said. She held the 's' when she said my name just a second longer than normal. The hand that shook mine was soft and strong. "They call me Vienna."

"It's a pleasure," I said, feeling a little starstruck.

"You can go, Lucas. Thanks for cleaning him up for me."

Lucas shrunk into the shadows and Vienna led me through the entryway to the front room where she sat me on an ornate couch that looked as if it had been looted from a museum. A steaming kettle sat on a tray beside me. She poured the water into a teacup and handed it to me.

"No, thank you," I said. "I just had coffee."

"It's herbal tea," she said. "Lavender. A purification herb."

"I need purification?" I joked.

"Don't we all? Especially after a stint in jail."

I laughed, but she only offered a slight smile in return.

"I'm typically quite blunt," she said. "The usual social norms can get in the way, sometimes. I like to get acquainted with the new arrivals quickly."

"So I've heard."

This time the smile was wide enough to show teeth.

"How well do you know our customs?"

"Just what I picked up around the bonfire tonight."

"Tell me."

She sat closer, raking the hair on the nape of my neck with her fingers.

"Your followers gave you a good report card is all," I said.

"Oh, they're not followers. We're all the same here."

"I don't think that's completely true."

I saw movement in the corner of the room. A python was winding up a wooden lattice made of smoothed logs, tongue flicking. I drank the tea and watched it rise toward the ceiling, Vienna playing with my hair all the while. My eyes felt heavy, and I felt an urge to rest my head on her lap and sleep.

"Tell you what, Steve. Why don't I show you the chapel room where we can lay down and rest our eyes awhile. It might be a long night. You're going to need your strength."

"Where's the chapel room?"

"Just at the end of the hall."

She took my hand and led me to a door trimmed with thick redwood lumber, strange glyphs and markings lacquered into the wood. Inside, a bed sat in a large wooden frame with more markings across the headboard, benches built into every wall. At the far end, the statue of a bearded man loomed with arms outstretched as if holding something invisible in his stony hands. I smelled lavender, along with the scent of candle smoke.

"Who's that supposed to be?" I asked.

"That's Andromalius."

"Andrew-what?"

"Andromalius. He is the serpent bearer. The center of our life here in the redwoods. The wellspring of our strength and fortune." She climbed onto the bed and smoothed the bedsheet with the palm of her hand. "Take your shoes off and lay with me."

I sat on the edge of the bed and tugged at the heels of my shoes, but lost my balance and fell to the floor. I felt numb all over and couldn't get steady no matter how hard I tried. Vienna held out her hand. I took it and she pulled me up, sat me back on the bed. She slipped off my shoes as I lay staring at the ceiling, eyes blurring and sharpening like a camera lens.

"Did you put something in my tea?"

My voice sounded sloppy, and I could barely get the words out.

"No, dear," she said. She looked almost angelic beside me, those hypnotic green eyes gently unknitting my bones as I melted into the bed. "You just had too much to drink."

"How do you do it?" I asked.

"How do I do what?"

"Become a cult leader?"

She was running her fingers up and down my chest. The room began to spin.

"I'm not a cult leader. Just one of the group."

My tongue went numb.

"Jus' tell me."

"I don't know, Steve. How does one become anything? Fate, ambition? All I know is I'm here for a reason, and that reason becomes more or less important depending on the circumstances. Right now it is very important. Supremely important."

I felt like I was passing out.

"And who is Andrew—"

"Andromalius," she said. "Keep up with me, now."

She sounded annoyed, impatient. I was vaguely aware that the sex I was expecting wasn't going to happen.

"What's his deal, then?"

"I'm sure you haven't read the Goetia, the Lesser Key of Solomon." She was talking down to me, now. "Since you don't know, I'll tell you. Andromalius is a fallen angel, last of the mighty Earls of Hell."

It was the last thing I heard before I drifted off, and when I opened my eyes again, the room was full of people. They sat on the low benches surrounding the bed, eyes closed as if meditating. I tried to sit up, but my body was too weak and I could only manage to hang one leg off the bed. Vienna stood over me, placed my leg back where it was before.

"Relax," she said. "Don't fight it."

The others whispered in unison, some language I couldn't make out. It didn't even sound real, like some crazy made-up words. I tried to sit up again, but whatever she'd given me left me almost completely paralyzed. My protests came out as quiet moans, and the group only whispered louder the more I tried.

The room spun, and at first I thought it was my head. But I could hear small castors chirping beneath the bed, the walls passing before me. When it stopped, I was facing the large statue of the bearded man. Those marble hands reaching, eyes staring down at me, through me.

My stomach cramped. The pain welled up into my throat and subsided. It came in waves, a sharp pain deep in my gut that moved up my throat and back down again. The chanting swelled to a loud, unbreakable chorus. It drowned any sound I managed to clear my lips. At the next wave of agony, my throat sealed up. I felt my back arch, body seize. Something was climbing up my throat, and without seeing it, I knew exactly what it was. I could feel the tongue flicking at the roof of my mouth, scales grinding along my esophagus as it moved.

The room tunneled.

Just the statue now—everything else hung in a shadowy vignette.

A snake's head emerged from my mouth, covered in mucous. It stretched darkly into the room like some creeping jungle vine, swiveling left to right, tasting the air as it grew ever longer. Just as the vignette closed and my vision faded to a graveyard black, the snake's tail came slithering from my throat. I heaved, turned on my side. This time, my breath was loud enough to overcome the chanting. I gasped and choked, pitched up on my elbows. The snake was winding up the statue now, around the bearded one's waist, inching along the arms until it found those reaching hands and draped itself there.

I rolled off the bed onto the floor, coughing blood.

"It's normal for your esophagus to tear a little," said Sheila. She sat closest to me, watching intensely. "Don't worry, the worst is over."

My legs wouldn't work, but I found I could pull myself along the ground in an army crawl. I reached for the door handle, and on the third try it creaked open. Nobody tried to stop me as I elbowed out of the room and down the hall toward the front door. I'd crawl all the way down the mountain if I had to, all the way into town on my hands and knees to get away if that's what it would take.

By the time I reached the driveway, the others had filtered out of the house and gathered around me. They came with their snakes, one after the other, moving with me as I wormed in the cold dirt. I pushed myself to my knees, blood gathering on my chin.

"What now?" I wheezed. "You gonna kill me?"

It hurt to talk. My throat felt full of razor blades.

"Now you have a choice," said Vienna. "You can stay and join us, or you can return to your sad city life. Whatever you choose is up to you, but you are forever bound to your familiar."

"My familiar?"

The long black snake I'd coughed up slithered over my thighs.

"The snake is a gift from Andromalius, last Earl of Hell."

"You can have it," I said. "I'm a dog person, anyway."

"Not anymore, you're not," said Vienna. "It will follow you to the ends of the earth. You and your familiar will be accepted at our compound. No one will question your bond."

I looked up at the group, all of them standing over me, white robes glowing eerily in the moonlight.

"Take me home," I said. "Or I'll crawl home."

"That's not the choice most people make."

"Well, I ain't most people."

‡

I don't know if the snake would have followed me to the ends of the earth, but it definitely followed me to Ocean Street. I came home after an all-day job search and found it coiled on my kitchen counter, flicking its little tongue. As much as I tried, I couldn't get rid of it. I started letting it go farther away from town but it came back every night.

Thing is, the longer it stayed with me, the better my luck changed.

I landed a job wrenching at the dealership on 41st Avenue. They gave me a good deal on a used car, too. The District Attorney's Office reduced my charges to misdemeanors and I won enough money at the downtown poker club to pay off my DUI fines. I even quit drinking so damn much. Soon, I stopped trying to ditch the snake and learned to live with it. I started feeding it rodents from the pet store, and that's when everything really started to click. Tax refunds, winning lottery tickets. Some days I felt like I just couldn't lose. Sure, the snake and I were bound by some Satanic woodland ceremony. But as time passed, it seemed to matter less.

After a year, I received a postcard from Vienna.

I was living in a much nicer apartment on the Westside, but they'd managed to track me down anyway. I wasn't really surprised about that part. What surprised me was how I felt when I saw the photo. All of them standing under the redwood tree, bearing serpents. Smiling and waving to the camera. I'd grown fond of my snake and it wasn't something I could explain to anyone else.

But they understood.

I took a photo with the snake on my shoulders and mailed it to them, and on the back I wrote that I might visit someday soon. Maybe I would, maybe I wouldn't.

Maybe I just needed a little time to come around.

Time to appreciate the Earl of Hell's gift for what it was.

A harbinger of very good things.

C.W. Blackwell is an American author from the Central Coast of California. His recent short stories have appeared with Reckon Review, Shotgun Honey, Tough Magazine, Rock and a Hard Place Magazine, and Fahrenheit Press. He is a 2021 Derringer award winner and 2022 finalist. His fiction novellas *Song of the Red Squire* and *Hard Mountain Clay* are available where books are sold.

THE HITMAN FROM HAZARD

Ashley Erwin

A handle-bar-mustache-crowning a shitty
fucking grin just double dawg daring Six Finger
Leander to make a fucking move is where we open.
Hand Grenade Harry, a hard killer from Hobb Holler
who packed a right proper parcel of guns wherever he
were like to go and who carried upon his personage
the exact *culprit* of every'thang to fall apart in the
after. A dick.

The transition to derision born in that very same
broke down barreled out building on the back lot of
Wynona Daily's land likewise known as a shawny,
which were where men'd go when they got done
swarpping, which set up shop in the land of drinking
and'a womanizing.

And on this fine, fair occasion, the celebratory corralling of likeminded lads, there were a re-groupment at work as sets of seedy seditions sawmilled on the floor in silence where unbeknownst to the current crew leader of the lot, that being Hand Grenade Harry, and his vigilante redneck-rat-pack were about to the get the dirty dawg double cross.

Players list out as such: Six Finger Leander and Dirty Dick Sanders, who were both northstar guided by the newly evolved notion that they were about to get away with something. That thousand-watt bulb beating dead body dense overtop 'em missing the train station connect entirely, as this weren't ever gonna play out as they planned.

But fast and mean and full up on fire, they were, and they made their early victories known with the following on the night before…

Dirty Dick Sanders, who got his name from a lack of washing as opposed to doubling down pipe to the town's misses, Jack Palance'd out, "Brothers, it's a simple bait and switch. Money's going to hit and I got an insider on the scene who's aimed to help us. She were right primed for the picking, boys.

Heist Day

The Gold Star Standard Bank positioned at the top of High Hazard Hill, where a measly drop of $10,000 is getting withdrawn from a vault by Filthy Tom, a local ne're-do-weller and the thick-boned cutie-pie raw-dawging gum who'd locked the box, Maggie.

What unlikely known at the time, was it all a little too late. For, not twenty-two minutes prior to Filthy Fucking Tom's prompt proposal and arrival at the bank, there would be the first turning of the screw. Six Finger Leander positioned in the power seat of a Gray Ford 350 delivered the dirty little rasher of news to Tip-top-Mcgoo-Tom there that he was in fact getting the old frame job. And Tom being notorious for any tattle-tale-tendril thrown his way decided that a dummy case to be introduced, i.e. Bag # 1.

However, in the "Where's the meat," moment of how big this little sammy's gonna be, one must actually go back exactly forty-four minutes to the women's restroom inside The Gold Standard Bank for hold-the-phone-betrayal-#2, where thick-boned cutie-pie-MAGGIE was in the middle of something not quite so cute as it apparently evident she was in fact lactose intolerant despite her adamant refusal to acknowledge such injustices; this particular episode playing fiddle in the second to last stall…ice cream..and though, one would hope and pray, most like, these discouragements left to solitude, she was not alone, for just as the final flush and waft of Poo-Porrii left a refreshingly citrus curtain of lemony zest, a pair of steel toe'd reinforced skull crushers hit the floor SCREAM-style next to her and out popped Six Finger Leander with a head full of ideas all his own. Specifically, the part where he says, "There's gonna be a decoy bag. Make sure the one with green lands."

But in this infinite merry-go-round-nature of who would betray whom, the felling of that first tree can only be with Maggie, for were it not slipped from her very mouth eighty-eight minutes prior while she was having said ice cream at Dusty's Dip-and-Stick with none other than Wynona Daily, where it solidified that she was in fact turn #3.

Per-xactly that moment when the bad blood first bled for Filthy Fucking Tom and Hand Grenade Harry. Not a week prior when the sun were just willing to set and the hellfire heat were clipping down the tip-back of a sixer in a body of water 'til yar eyeballs brim-yeller-rimmed-right and yar fingers all good-bbq-crinkle-fry'd, where Filthy Fucking Tom were looking forward to rectifying just that and just as he'd

Parked

Sat

Fridgerator

Stacked a set of good-n-frosties 'fore him on that dark wood table that piggyback rode atop some brown shag carpet smelling just like every butt big-mack-smacked inside that lime green dollar general ashtray there were, a rappy-tap-tap on the door.

Hand Grenade Harry with a fresh from the daisies glossy glow and a sack full of promises he'd every intention of not keeping, including the cut of whatever sold, and in true form hurriedly helped hisself to a beer without the ask nor tale sending Filthy Fucking Tom into a boiled cauldron of cracked craniums that would need dealt with soon.

Amongst the many things Hand Grenade Harry had not counted on when calling that evening on Filthy Fucking Tom was the primary conniving complication of the already awaiting compatriot in the back room, who had a plan all their own.

Wynona Daily, motivated by her own compulsion and the imminent knowhow that this would not bare fruitful form any longer, plus a lust for life renewed by a dip in the Maggie lady pond did what any ordinary woman would do—went searching for the dynamite switch. And low and behold, in a lip locked fantasy play of what might come next, a velveteen gift served on a memory.

"Ya ever dream of leaving?" Wynona asks with a fiddled curl wrapped right round her ring finger.

"Every fucking day," Maggie Virginia-slimmed out.

"Wouldn't take all that much money, ya know," Wynona says steeling a drag. "Couple of thousand, enough to disappear but not so much to call attention."

"Well there ain't a lot money in this town, honeybun. Except…" Maggie stops shy, rolling on her side to face Wynona. "Ya know who has the strangest superstition and more money than he's got sense. Ever heard of the legend of the White Buffalo?"

It should be noted that amongst Filthy Fucking Tom's many attributes, superstition, women, and investments were at times all tied up in one. And as he himself was parlaying the legend of his most ungettable get to a one Miss-Cutie-Pie-bank-teller-Maggie post coital many moons ago, he shared the Legend of the White Buffalo.

"Up in the hollers by a stream, the White Buffalo is said to appear and if you ever give cause to happen upon her, good fortune to follow. But the White Buffalo don't come alone. There's two handlers, one can be bought and the other cannot."

"So how do you know," Maggie asks.

"You don't," he clipped.

Two months later, Wynona Daily's get out of jail free card came when she called into the Big Dipper radio show, a show which everyone in Eastern Kentucky lived by, and on said evening whilst folks were preparing themselves for a nighty-night, the following played out.

"Hello caller, you're on the Dipper Show."

"The White Buffalo Waits."

"Mam, I'm afraid I don't know what that means."

Per-xactly, the illusion of the phrase not meant for the Big Dipper, but moreso to the fast on his feet Dirty Dick Sanders, who lept from his bed with a panic in his eye and danger in his head, his lips slipping need for a $10,000 fat rack and a place in the country to be.

Lunchtime…with half the bank tellers off…Maggie makes her way back to the post-op with Six Finger Leander's words burning coal in her ears: "Bag # 1 goes in BOX 3495XTP. Bag #2 goes in the bin."

Meanwhile, outside in a beat to shit Ford Explorer, the Hyenas of the Hill: Hand Grenade Harry, Six Finger Leander, and Dirty Dick Sanders serving straight creepy crawlers.

Their sight pointed to Filthy Fucking Tom and his sweaty palms manhandling two cases in double digit humidity walking into the bank with a bee-line straight for thick-boned Maggie waiting at the bank door.

In clippety-clap-back to slap stacks…the car doors open…the masks pulling down…and as the Hyenas of the Hill nudge their way after Tom, a misunderstanding ensues.

Six Finger Leander, busy carving butcher knives in the back of Hand Grenade Harry's head, was paying far too little attention to his footsteps below and tottered into the back of Dirty Dick Sanders. A no fault to his own. But little-ricky-tick-DICK-there didn't take too kindly to an unwarranted bump and a rebuttal soon to erupt. Which forced Hand Grenade Harry to try and break-up the children from play which led to a knife and then a Billy Club surreptitiously pulled from a place unbefitting its holding and then a gun and then another gun and then masks pulled off and then one on one, and two on two, cursing in the street, and an all altogether rather messy show of biting and kicking and fighting and licking, which was weird because there wasn't really a need for that, and it rather off-putting to the small gaggle of folks coming back to punch the clock after their mid-week nourishment, you can imagine…grown men…fighting in the street…and in between the jabs and ear pulling and the weird kitty slapping that was happening between Dirty Dick Sanders and Six Finger Leander with little paws of winded fat men unable to find their footing until…dreadfully so…Six Finger Leander took a Haymaker right to the gut and toddler spewed right there where he stood….it was just truly gawdawful…at least one would think…but then the slip-n-slide that occurred from the juices…Jesus…that was not meant to be viewed in a public forum…BUT at least Hand Grenade Harry kept his tail on Filthy Tom and got in the bank …so there's that.

However if like me, you're in the business of not just knowing what you're feasting on but where that feast rears its pretty head before the slaughter, the full jump-off begins a fortnight ago, where, heavily invested in the re-runs of Golden Girls and everyone's favorite floozy, Blanche, Six Finger Leander was beckoned by yet another rappy-tap-tap on his door. And who pre-tell should be waiting that other side of trailer park galore with the going rate of services soon to be rendered, the always agreed upon: 1 carton of Marlboro Reds, 1 sixer of Blue Label Sodas, one stack of fresh-from-the-stretch Jacksons numbering in the per head allotment of $5,000 but Filthy Fucking Tom, hisself.

Seemed Hand Grenade Harry had gotten handsy with the wrong honey, a thick little cutie-pie called Maggie and upon her confession to Filthy Fucking Tom with great and fastidious remorse where words like, "Daddy" dripped from her lips, the proposition put in practice. And being that Six Finger Leander just as down right and dirty as Filthy Tom gave a head nod and waited for the players to come to him. For a hired hand is after all a hired hand.

A simple-triple-bait-and-switch.

Six Finger Leander cured and charged standing inside the bank rotunda with the timing 'bout right, that extra thumb of his looped in a sling of metal that's packing a supercharged Long Nose 41 that'd shoot the wings off a tick at 100 yards if he hadn't took no drink, which he hadn't.

Tangentially, an elevator door Dracula-counting-1-2-3 is shoving gravity to the main floor from the basement carrying Filthy Fucking Tom and thick-hipped-Maggie up from a job well done where both are holding fast two twin black bags. And as if the bench not stacked enough, an interloper on the scene, a one Ms. Wynona Daily making "an innocent deposit" as Dirty Dick Sanders takes a long hard looksee at the near empty room 'cept for them and a snaggletooth speckling of tellers.

The key to the capture-the-flag game was Six Finger Leander had every intention of shooting Hand Grenade Harry, grabbing both bags off Filthy Fucking Tom and lovey-dove-Maggie, cradling past Dirty Dick Sanders with a bullet somewhere landed therein, and hopping right back in his beat to shit Ford Explorer and hightailing it outta there. But life's got different plans and in this dastardly derisive display of downright mean, Hand Grenade Harry popped off with a full on I'll-be-your-Huckleberry shot to a stained-glass window just behind Leander there. Letting all loosey-goosey a deluge of glass shards over all the room then portended a particularly politicized pile-drive overtop Leander with the butt of his gun.

Which had that been the end, Six Finger Leander could've very well just pulled the trigger and shot. But, alas, Dirty Dick Sanders didn't care very much for the absurdist interruption to his plan, which were to shoot Six Finger Leander there, grab light-of-my-life-Maggie and set off in the sunset with $10,000 large to live the rest of their days together. And all that got kicked to shit right quick when Wynona Daily decided it time to pull arson into this little scenario here and ripped from her purse a mason jar of kerosene 'cause ain't not one got their noggin screwed on right and started throwing liquid on Six Finger Leander and Dirty Dick Sanders and following up with the lighting of a match. Indoors.

Which clearly sent a turn in the road for it was not Hand Grenade Harry's intention to handle it this way nor did he particularly appreciate his wife's contributions to the two flailing fire geysers of Dirty Dick Sanders and Six Finger Leander and just as Filthy Fucking Tom looked on in crazed amaze with a set of roadrunners wishing for a getaway, cute little Maggie donned her Cindi Lauper'd True Colors moment and from under her skirt, pulled the infamous pea-shooter that she shoved into the side of Filthy Fucking Tom there and sent that meet-your-maker-moment right through the femoral. Then grabbing the black bag with a toss towards Miss. Wynona Daily, she heavy-chevy'd after Hand Grenade Harry in a 3-point stance only Lawrence Taylor could've pulled off and knocked that motherfucking into next week.

The Hitman from Hazard's eyes were still closed when Maggie and Wynona crunched over glass. He was out for the count. The tellers, what'd stayed around, were crunched up under a desk daring not even a possum peak at the two women unzipping bags with a double check, and as the both of them left, Wynona bent down for a surprise souvenir . At her feet a somewhat intact piece of the stained-glass window Hand Grenade Harry'd shot through.

"Maggie, is that a gawdamned White Buffalo?"

"Sure enough is, sugar. Now, let's boot-scoot-n-boogie on out of here."

Ashley Erwin is the Southern Pulp writer of *Grit, Black, Blood* and *A Ballad Concerning Black Betty or the Retelling of a Mankiller and Her Machete*, with shorts appearing in Cheap Pop, Shotgun Honey, Switchblade, Revolution John, and Cowboy Jamboree's 'Grotesque Art." An avid reader at Noir at the Bar traveling across the country with some jaunts over the pond for debauchery in England, she is the Woman to a Man and the holder of a fat cat named Booboo and she bides her time in sunny Los Angeles peddling whiskey.

Sticky Stuff

Nils Gilbertson

You dream about it as a kid. Saturday afternoons spent smacking whiffle balls over the fence into the neighbor's yard, mimicking the crowd's roar, scampering around the weeds and cracked concrete slabs onto chalk-drawn bases. But a boy's imagination is a hell of a thing—avoiding tags and line shots instead of rusted lawnmowers and tangled hoses. The smell doesn't emanate from the overflowing trash bins, but rather from the infield dirt and fresh-cut grass. It wasn't cheap plastic in my hands, but a calloused grip on finely-stitched seams. Back then, all I thought of was now. Now, all I think of is then. Memories of a dream come and gone. In my boyhood, playing big league ball was all I'd ever wanted, the foul lines delineating Heaven from Hell. And there was nothing better than the All-Star Game. Now, a few decades later, the ol' Midsummer Classic sounded like a pain in the ass. Play in this league long enough and you'd get it. Shit, live long enough, even Heaven starts to sound like an unnecessary extension of consciousness. Extra innings. Things ought to end when they end.

Still, I looked forward to the All-Star break, precisely because I never made the cut. What was better than five days where I didn't have to show my face at the ballpark? No spot starts or long relief gigs to eat up innings? No treatment on my throbbing elbow? I plopped the shot glass into the beer and put back the boilermaker with a steep tilt of the icy mug.

I waved Val, the bartender at Striker's Pub, down to the end of the bar.

"Give me a Budweiser. And turn off that damn Home Run Derby. Or mute it, at least. Glorified batting practice is all it is."

Val grinned as though she'd never quite learned how. "Getting PTSD watching the sluggers, huh, Mitch?"

I grunted and shooed her away. Looking up at the TV, I felt bad for the assholes on the glowing screen. It was tough to think of a worse fate for a ballplayer than having to travel to some shit city, make small talk with league-mates, and pitch an inning to get shelled by the best hitters in the league. Sounded like a bad deal to me. Even worse, they'd soon encounter the dull ache of the hangover from accomplishing one's dreams. Dedicate your life to reaching something, the worst thing that can happen is to get it. Once you do, there's nothing left. The heat of competition shines bright and can spurn you forward for years. But, like all passions, it flickers and dies. When it's gone, it's gone. Nothing to fill the void.

But what the hell did I know. As a mediocre spot starter who'd spent most of his twenties bouncing back and forth between the bigs and the farm system, I never got the invite. Never would. Now I was in my mid-thirties, taking pain pills and getting injections to numb my arm enough to pitch, one injury or a few bad outings away from never getting another contract. Not to mention bitter as gas station coffee. I was a free agent at the end of the season, and a new deal, even a modest one, would be nice. Good to stay in one place for my last few years. Before landing with the Waynesport Diablos, I'd been passed around the league like a two-dollar whore. You start feeling like a commodity. And not a sought-after commodity that makes ESPN headlines; I was a bargaining chip tossed in for salary balance. A general manager's afterthought, doing what he can to make the deal square.

A few more beers in, I noticed a couple of drunk fellas towards the other end of the bar who were doing their best to whisper and point without me noticing. The place was empty except for us, and Val had relented and muted the festivities, so I got the gist of their not-so-subtle gestures. One of them stumbled over at the other fella's urging. He donned the familiar crimson and gray jersey. Kent Perkins, number 21. Our ace.

"Hey, man, don't mean to be a bother," he slurred. "You're Mitch Ward, right? Of the Diablos?"

I shrugged and waved to Val to keep them coming. "Diablos? Never heard of 'em."

He looked back at the friend, as though asking for help. "C'mon, man. I know it's you. We won't be a bother. Only wanted to say hey, and how 'bout a playoff push?"

"Thanks, kid. Now that I've heard it from you, I'll do my damndest."

He stared at me, mouth open, leaning on the bar to keep himself steady. I could feel the heat of his whiskey breath.

"Hell, Mitch," Val said, serving me my next drink. "No need to be a prick about it. Better enjoy the fans while you still have any."

I sighed and tried to shake the instinct that if I spread misery around, it might decide to leave me alone. But misery wasn't a fixed sum; there could always be more. Even worse, I'd inherited a rotten, festering flavor of misery. I felt it—smelled it—leaking from my pores. It was laced with guilt. I was so damn well off, considering. Better than most people on earth, most people in history. What right did I have to be miserable?

"Sorry, guy," I said. "Playoff push, got it. I'll pass the word along to your guy, Perkins, too. Hey, you got a Sharpie on you? I can fake his signature real good. Could make you a few hundred bucks, at least."

That sent him on his way. Val couldn't help but laugh. "Haven't seen someone spot you in the wild like that in a while," she said. "Might be the last time."

"I wish."

‡

City lights on the rippling bay and cold wind numbing my cheeks made the past and future vanish. It was good to feel. Sometimes I was grateful for the aches and pains. Other times—after a pill and a six-pack—numbness was the greatest comfort, nothingness the natural state of things. All sensation was an anomaly, a blip on the eternal radar.

Striker's Pub was housed in an old shack at the foot of the bay, in the shadow of the stadium. It got by with its cult-following old-timers and kids who spent their salaries on overpriced studio apartments and thus couldn't afford the ten-dollar beers served at the trendy spots on stadium row. During the off-season I spent most nights at the place, each time making the cold, lonesome walks back to my high-rise apartment on the other side of the stadium. Couldn't do it during the season. We were either on the road, or, for home games, too many folks around. The die-hards would recognize me.

The All-Star break provided a reprieve, and I took advantage. I stumbled along the high brick wall on the outside of the right-field bleachers. It was a scenic walkway, the stadium on one side, ice-cold water on the other. I cursed at the thought that I'd only let one batter hit a splash shot off me the couple of years prior. First half of this season, there'd already been three.

It was a funny thing to be thirty-five and on the verge of losing your livelihood—the craft you'd dedicated your life towards. Soon to be gone, forgotten. All I ever did was pitch. At every other level, I was the best there was. I turned my back on family, friends, love, everything. My purpose was to hurl a ball, and I embraced it. But, once you get to the pros, you realize how far from the best you are. And when your career starts winding down, you become ordinary, verging on useless. Like an old man losing his faculties. Sure, the money's good, and the celebrity of it made you feel better than you ought to. In my younger days, I'd go out with teammates to the bars and clubs, and bringing a gal home was a can of corn. That lifestyle runs its course. I looked out to the bridge jutting from the city, the dull rush of traffic reminding me of the passage of time. I'd be out of the league in a couple of years with no skills and no one who gave a damn. Funny how, in the stadium lights, having nothing could look like having it all. I went to the ledge and spat into the mild swells. My sweaty hands were slick on the cold railing. I thought how easy it was to lose my grip—to watch it all slip away. Nothing to break my fall. At least it wasn't too far a drop.

‡

The next morning, I went on what I charitably called a run. Then I met up with Rick, a trainer for the Diablos who worked with the pitchers. He was about as sharp as a baseball but I didn't care much. Better company than most of my teammates. Gave a hell of an elbow massage. On off days, we'd meet for a bite and then head in for treatment.

"You watch the Derby last night?" he asked, shoveling egg whites into his mouth. He tried to slurp the last few morsels of runaway egg but they dribbled into his beard.

"Did my best not to."

"Don't blame ya. Those boys can rip. Best to spend this time getting your mind right. You know, after your last outing?"

"Sure, Rick. Thanks for reminding me."

"All good. Now forget about it. Short memory."

I sipped my coffee and felt the creeping dread of my next start. That's all it brought me anymore. Pain and dread. Pitching was a mental game more than anything; the trick was not getting too high or too low. When you did, getting back to basics was key. In my younger days, it was pure nature. My mind would understand that the body and soul had taken over and would shut down for the duration. For those nine innings, I was the center of the universe, everything moving at my pace. I was a God— or at least covering His night shift. It was the only time in my life I'd ever been in control. Over time, the invincibility I felt on the rubber faded and I did too. Left in my wake was a man afraid that not even the mirror would look back.

"I don't know, Rick. Sometimes I feel like I'm losing it out there." I liked opening up to a dummy like Rick. Good to get the thoughts out without expecting anything in return.

"Out on the mound?"

"On the mound, in life, everywhere. It's slipping away. I'm losing my youth, my skill, everything I hang my hat on. I try to hold on, but I can't. Like I'm losing my grip on nothing." I felt his blank stare. "See, I keep having this dream where I'm about to fall off a cliff, but I'm hanging onto the rail. My hand is slipping and when it does, I fall for a while, screaming. I'm able to grab onto something, but it's the same all over again. Until the last one."

"Then you wake up?"

"No. Then I die."

Rick kept staring for a while, then started clicking his tongue as though trying to jump-start his brain. "Well, shit, man. If you're having grip problems, we can work that out."

‡

Even though I blended into a bar crowd like a drunk chameleon, I hid in a corner booth at Striker's that night. The place was as full as I'd ever seen it for the All-Star Game. I forced myself to watch as I put the drinks back. Some sort of punishment for never climbing that mountain. Each time I got up to go to the can, I felt the pill bottle in my pocket—its rattle a siren song. I stood at the urinal and eyed the stall. Crush and inhale. The narcotics begged to swim through my bloodstream, awash in the booze. The two sure knew how to bring out the best in each other. How can you say no to friends like that?

When I got back to the booth, a fresh boilermaker was ready and waiting. I grinned at my superior league-mates on the screen. I knew what awaited them. Even after a night of adulation and waving their caps to adoring fans, tomorrow would offer nothing more than yesterday.

In the fifth inning, Val stopped bringing the periodic drinks I'd requested. Breathing seemed to require conscious exertion, the slow exhale tickling my nose hairs. I sunk into myself and the rest of the bar sagged and melted like a collapsing dream. A sneeze brought me back and I realized it was my own. As I rubbed my swollen eyes and glanced around, the bar had emptied, except for a man sitting across from me.

I ignored him for a few minutes, a lingering vestige of a fantasy that would fade into the neon-lit barroom. But Val came over and smiled at the man and then at me and said, "Oh good, you found a friend." Back to him. "What can I get ya?"

"Old Pal, darling."

She nodded and turned to me and said, "Enough of the hard stuff for you. I'll get you a beer."

The man reached into the pocket of his sport coat and pulled out a baseball like a magic trick. He rolled it across the table. I grabbed it on instinct.

"How does that feel?" he asked, grinning. He was bald with a neatly trimmed mustache and olive skin that gleamed in the bar light.

"Feels like a baseball."

"It is a baseball."

I examined it. "Sure is. What're you peddling, cue ball?"

His laugh was sharp at the edges. "Mr. Ward, it's my understanding that you've had some issues on the mound that I can help you with."

"You selling time machines?"

That one only got a grin out of him. "Give me your hand."

"Why in hell would I do that?"

He stared at me as though he knew that I would, so I did. Right then, Val came with our drinks. "Aw, you fellas make a cute pair."

"Jesus. Thanks, Val."

The man pulled out a small, unlabeled tin canister with his free hand. He flipped the cap off with a steady thumb, rubbed an index finger in the clear balm inside, and wiped it on the back of my hand.

"Try it."

"The hell you mean try it? You selling lotion?" But I knew it wasn't. I felt its stickiness. My skin tingled.

"Try it with the ball," he said.

I dabbed the fingers of my left hand on the spot on my right wrist where he'd smeared the substance. They, too, tingled, almost to the point of numbness. He sensed this and said, "Give it a moment." As the feeling faded, I gripped the ball. It was nothing like I'd ever felt. Even with the booze and pain pills dulling my senses, the seams molded to my fingers, the leather synchronizing with my flesh. I gripped a four-seamer. Loose, but firm. Sticky. It felt so damn good I would've bet my firstborn that I could hurl it clear across the bay.

But a wave of lucidity washed away the excitement. I peeled the ball from my hand and rolled it back to him. Somehow, my fingers weren't sticky, only dampened with sweat in the stuffy barroom. "Don't you know the league's cracking down on this shit?" I said. "They barely let us use pine tar anymore. And the checks they're doing now between innings? Umps are acting like the goddamn TSA. I mean, I get it. You fellas have cracked the formula that'll ratchet up my spin rate. But they've figured it out. You're a little late to the party."

I could tell he'd heard it before and was waiting for me to shut my mouth. When I did, his eyes wandered to the empty bar and found their way back to me. "This formula? No. This formula is like no other. I could see it in your eyes the moment it met your fingers. Any pitcher worth his salt doesn't need to throw a single bullpen pitch to know it."

I shook my head. "Even so, they're cracking down on it. It's not like it used to be."

He tugged on an earlobe and brushed his shoulder as though giving a sign. Then, again, on the other side. He looked down at my empty hands as I gripped my beer bottle. "How does it feel now?"

I downed half the beer, put it down, and probed the spot where he'd applied the stuff. Only sweat.

"It's undetectable," he said. "Sticky only when first applied and when it comes into contact with both your skin and the baseball. If left on your hand, it blends with your sweat. But when you grab the ball, it retains its adhesive qualities. It's not goopy, nor does it leave noticeable residue on the ball. Invisible."

We paused as Val came back over. "Can I get you fellas a couple more?"

"Sure," I said. "He's buying."

The man smiled and nodded. "It's my pleasure."

"Invisible, huh?" I said after Val went back to the bar. "And how do you make this magical gunk?"

"Don't worry about that. Are you interested?"

"Slow down, stranger. I haven't even thrown so much as a damn bullpen session with it. And I didn't catch your name, either."

He slid a card across the bar.

"Card, huh? Old school. And what's the catch if I would happen to want to get my hands on some of this stuff?"

"No catch at all. It's yours for the rest of the season." He paused and I waited. "If you make the most of the product and sign a lucrative off-season contract, we would receive a modest cut."

"And if I burn out?"

"Then no payment at all. Like so many, Mr. Ward, I'm a man who enjoys rooting for the underdog. To hell with aces and stars and young prospects. In you, I see a man in the gutter—someone worth helping. Worth rehabilitating. Only if I can do that, do you owe me."

I thought it over and tipped my beer towards him. "Keep these coming and we'll get along fine."

‡

The dream was different that night. I was on a glass-bottom boat out on the bay. In the beginning, there was nothing to look at, the water too murky to see into the underworld. But the captain—the bald man—took us to a small cove where the water was bright aqua, like some tropical paradise. We floated onto the spot. The bald man said, "Take a look."

There were no fish or other wonders of the sea below the glass. Rather, we were looking down into the pits of Hell. The others in the boat laughed, mocking the eternal suffering of the damned as they roasted. I pleaded for them to stop, but they grabbed ahold and threw me overboard. Then I was drowning in flames, fighting to break the glass from below.

Then I was drenched in sunlight. My head throbbed and my mouth was stale. I turned over and cursed consciousness until it gave up on me and I fell back asleep. But the extra hour of rest couldn't repave the path towards the previously uncharted corners of my subconscious. When I woke up again it was eleven in the morning, the sun high in the sky, shining through the large sky-rise windows. Boats crossed the bay's shimmering surface, foam lines rippling in their wake. It felt like penance.

The bad mornings, I skipped the pills and let hurt fill the emptiness. I welcomed the aches and quivers that ran through my exhausted muscles and abused organs. When it reached that unbearable throb, I tried to imagine what it would be like if it were immeasurably worse. How bad could pain get? Ever read some of the torture routines they used in the medieval days? Flaying you alive? Hanging you upside down and sawing you in half? One method was to make you drink milk and honey until you puked and shit out your innards. Then they'd send you out tied to a boat and let the birds and bugs gnaw at you as you decomposed. I couldn't imagine, but I tried to. Anything to put my petty twenty-first century pain into perspective.

There was a tin next to my keys and wallet on the floor. I gave my swollen brain a few minutes for the memories to come back. The man in the bar, the sticky stuff. Smears of recollection that it was a special formula, he was giving me a deal, it wouldn't get me caught by the league.

My mind's eye of the conversation was like a scratched DVD. Once we'd shaken hands and he said to hold onto the stuff, try it out, the feed went black.

I cracked the lid and dabbed my fingers in the goo. They began to tingle.

‡

Pitchers have been screwing with balls to get a leg up for as long as the game existed. Back in the day, there was the spitball. Get it good and slippery and the ball'd come dancing from your hand with a mind of its own. Over the years, pitchers realized to get a real advantage you wanted things sticky. *It's not about velocity—it's about spin rate* is how the analytics types would explain it. Get a better grip, it gets the ball spinning faster, which gives it more movement. Pitchers soon saw the results, and before long we were all doing it. And we didn't just want a leg up on the batters—we wanted it over pitchers. Pine tar and rosin and sunscreen wouldn't cut it because we all had it. Behind the scenes, teams hired scientists to come up with the perfect formula to max out our spin rate. It worked. Batting averages plummeted and the league started losing money. People don't want to watch a strikeout every other at-bat. Shit's boring. When the money started drying up, the moneymakers cracked down. Now, between innings, they might as well be checking for the stuff between our ass cheeks. Good for hitters, fine for the elite throwers, bad for guys like me.

Today it was different. Even after puking behind the bullpen rubber, I was throwing the best I had in a decade. The pop of the catcher's mitt, the sharp cut of the slider, the noticeable rise of the four-seamer.

After the session, I went up to Rick, who was grinning at the tracker. When my catcher walked up behind us to take a look, he almost spat his chew onto the screen.

"Jesus, Mitch," he said. "The hell's gotten into you today? That spin's insane."

I shrugged and nodded at Rick. "Guess I got a grip, is all."

‡

I called the number on the card I found in my jeans from the night before, and we made a deal. All the sticky stuff I needed for the rest of the season. If I got a contract at the end of the year that put me in the top half of pitchers' salaries league-wide—they would get a ten-percent cut for the duration of that contract. At my age, it was an insane deal on their part. Until I started pitching with their stuff.

The first few outings, nothing changed. Sure, I was pitching shutout innings and whiffing guys, but every big-league pitcher has good runs. It was a start on the road against the division leader a couple of weeks later that did it. Complete game two-hit shutout, twelve Ks. You could hear the collective *who the hell's this guy* mutters from the stunned crowd.

Between that and one of our starters tweaking his shoulder, it solidified me in the rotation. Before I knew it, I was putting up Cy Young numbers, had I not shat the bed in the first half of the season. You bet the league was getting suspicious. I was getting fondled by umps damn near every inning. I grinned and took it. The sticky stuff was invisible, but I wasn't anymore.

Best of all, the old feeling came back. I bathed in the previously forgotten sensation of being in control. I threw at batters for fun at rival stadiums, so I could step off the rubber and bask in the *boos*. The stadium was like its own universe with me at its center. Each pair of eyes on me, cheering or heckling, it didn't matter. Nothing happened unless I willed it into being—my windup like the rising sun. I no longer needed the bottle. The pills were too stubborn to leave, but I took them in a way that would make the team doctor proud. The mound was my sanctuary; it was all that I needed.

‡

We ended the year on a twelve-game win streak and stole the division crown. I'd get my contract, no question. But I wanted more.

Same as the pills and the drink, success is something you get numb to. Game one of the division series, Perkins did what aces do and we won 4-0. I was scheduled to start game two.

They were waiting in the living room when I woke up. He was sitting on the couch, the back of his head an orb of flesh reflecting the morning sun. It looked fake, pulled too tightly over his skull, like a mannequin. Two fellas stood in the corners, their stares reminding me how high up we were—how accidents happen.

He didn't turn to look at me as he started to speak. "Big start today, isn't it?" An intermittent clicking interrupting the vaguely familiar voice. When I crossed the apartment to stand in front of him, I saw that he was clipping his fingernails, brushing the remnants between the pillows.

"You mind?"

He frowned. "I'm sorry for making myself at home. After all that we've accomplished together, it's as though we're family. Don't you agree, Mr. Ward?"

"Sure, family. What the hell are you doing in my apartment?"

His face creased. He pocketed the clipper and started pacing the room, settling at the window, looking out at the views of the bay. "I hate to say it, but despite your success on the mound, we've grown nervous about our arrangement."

"How so? You give me the stuff, I get my contract at the end of the year, you get your cut. Deal's a deal."

He turned to face me. "That's right. A deal's a deal. That's why I'm here. You see, our deal extended through the end of the *regular* season. It's the playoffs now. We spoke nothing of playoffs before. We're here to renegotiate."

"Are you insane? I'm pitching the biggest game of my life tonight. You understand how much more money I'll make—we'll make—if I show up in the playoffs?"

He cleared his throat and eyed the wood-paneled floor. The fellas in the corners were statues.

"Our operation," he said, "has run into a bit of a problem. We need to correct it, and we need resources—money. Now."

"Operation? I don't give a shit about your operation. I got enough stuff here to get me through—"

"No. You don't."

I closed my eyes and breathed. The blackness turned into my bathroom and I swung open the bottom drawer and pulled out the toiletry bag hidden behind the pipes. Empty.

He said from the doorway, "You ought to give us what we need. For your own sake."

The turbulence of the moment leveled me. Who I'd been—who I was—how fast that can change. How fast everything can change and what little control we had. The floor began to oscillate and the walls extended upward and the ceiling vanished overhead, revealing the sky, the universe, above. In an act of defiance, I snatched a pair of scissors from the cabinet and went at him. But momentum swung me from my feet and I was at the bottom of the ocean, the leagues of sea between me and the surface swallowing any sliver of sunlight. I struggled until a voice assured me that it would be over soon. To let it be.

Then, shaken violently from the corners of my mind, I was back in my living room.

"What'd you say?"

He looked as though, wherever I'd gone, he'd gone with me.

"I said that you don't have any more sticky stuff. My colleagues made sure of that."

"I need it," I mumbled.

"Then we need help."

"The operation," I said, "let me see it."

"You don't want to see it, Mr. Ward."

"I'm not giving you shit till I see what you need money for. And I need the sticky stuff."

He nodded, turned back towards the window, and watched the slow crawl of life below. "Tell me, Mr. Ward, did you even find your way back onto the boat?"

"Excuse me?"

"The glass-bottom boat. You were trying so hard to escape, to crack that glass. Were you able to?"

"How the hell'd you—" Memories like water through fingers. At once, I felt all the lives I'd ever lived entangled in a knotted mass of regret. The night at the bar was a malfunctioning railway switch, cross-directing the fake and real, conscious and unconscious. The man before me was the conductor sending me on a path that was never meant to be—dreams inverted into living nightmares.

"Show me."

He sighed. "As you wish."

‡

I sat in the back of the black car as it slithered through downtown Waynesport towards the southern point of the city and a forgotten appendage called Cape Carlisle, better known as The Wasteland. Decades ago, it had been a bustling naval port. But a nuclear waste scare had condemned the place to an expanse of crumbling shipyard and hollowed-out buildings. Some artistic types had tried to revive it, ideal for urban artwork. But they soon learned that it wasn't completely abandoned. There were still congregations of those the rest of us were blind to.

We drove past the abandoned shipyard, further south. Deteriorating cranes overlooked the ghostly harbor. If it weren't for the luxurious homes dotting the hills beyond, it would have been a dystopian hellscape. Some Mad Max-type shit. There were even a few spray-painted wheel loaders, time and circumstance rendering them useless. Not even worth the effort to discard.

There was a container yard beyond the port. I could smell it before I saw the billowing lime-green smoke. Like inhaling gaseous rot. We parked out front of a warehouse and saw that the worst of the fire was over, the neon smog condensing into a sickly cloud overhead. When I opened the car door, the atmosphere was like biting down on burnt tinfoil.

"Jesus, take this." A man tossed me a gas mask. I turned around. My companions emerged from the car with theirs already on. The man said to them, "Make it quick, you don't want to be in there for more than ten minutes."

It looked like it used to be quite a lab. People in hazmat suits were sifting through the rubble. Blackened equipment and metal tables were half-melted, some unearthly substance having eaten through them. Dangling shards of scorched metal stabbed through the smoke. It felt as though the air was eating through my mask. But I kept going. Kept looking. As though for someone to tell me it was okay. Things would be okay. I heard muffled warnings but ignored them. Losing the others, I turned down a narrow hallway in the back corner of the warehouse. Screeches pierced through the hall and I hoped the source was some accidental chemical reaction. But it sounded too familiar. Too much like those like those suffering beneath the glass-bottom boat.

At the end of the hall, a door was ajar. Men in hazmat suits leaning over bodies. Stumps of limbs charred and blackened like tips of used matches. Still twitching. Incomprehensible garbles communicating that they no longer wanted to be.

"Do it," one of the intact men said.

A quivering pistol.

"Hold on, who the hell are you?"

I ran, back through the clouded hall, until I found a door that would open into the world. I slammed into it and crumpled onto the pavement outside. I vomited until they were dry heaves and dry-heaved until they found me.

"Now you see what we're dealing with," he said. "We can fix this with your help, get things back up and running. Back to normal." He leaned down next to me. The mask hung from his bald head and he looked like a giant insect. He pulled it off and showed his red, watering eyes. "We can even lower the cut we get from your contract. But we need help now. Or you don't know the shit you'll bring down on all of us. You especially." He paused to reach into his pocket. "Here, we salvaged some of the sticky stuff. Enough for the playoffs, even if you go to game seven of the World Series."

I looked down at the tin and thought of all the horrible things I'd done and the endless thread of consequences of even the not-so-horrible things. That's all we did—exist for a split second and leave a piss trail of destruction. All to get a better grip.

‡

It was a gorgeous night at the ballpark and the crowd was louder than ever. Playoff baseball was a hell of a thing. I rubbed some dirt on the fresh ball, then my fingers against the back of my neck. They began to tingle. I kept on working the ball and found the seams and toed the rubber. The crowd roared and I hurled the opening pitch.

Strike one!

Nils Gilbertson is a writer and attorney. He lives in Texas with his wife, son, and German Shorthaired Pointer. His short stories have appeared in Mystery Magazine, Mickey Finn: 21st Century Noir Vols. 2 & 3, Rock and a Hard Place, Mystery Tribune, Gone: An Anthology of Crime Stories, Cowboy Jamboree, and others. His story "Washed Up" was named a Distinguished Story in The Best American Mystery and Suspense 2022. You can find him at nilsgilbertson.com and on Twitter @NilsGilbertson.

Two Day Rental

Victor De Anda

West Los Angeles, CA. 1999

Orson Welles was twenty-three when he
directed *Citizen Kane*. My twenty-fifth
birthday's a month away, but my broke ass is
working in a video store until a real gig
comes along. You'd think a diploma from
USC would help, but so far, no dice. This
job's only temporary until the muse blesses
me with a hit screenplay. That bitch is a fickle
one, let me tell you.

It's a quiet Thursday afternoon at Cinematic when the cordless rings out like an alarm clock. A handful of customers stagger between the VHS and DVD racks like zombies in a Romero movie. Some look like film students, others like out of work actors and filmmakers. A few look familiar, but most of them are just nobodies.

They all come to Cinematic for the movies they can't find at Blockbuster or Hollywood Video. Talk to any movie geek in L.A. and they'll tell you we've got the best selection in town. I suppose there are worse places to work. Besides, as employees, we get free movie rentals.

The cordless rings again on the front counter. It's within reach, but my gut reaction's to let someone else answer it. Scott, our store manager is perched on his stool behind the cash register. The cordless rings again and he lowers the Premiere magazine he's been reading. His raised eyebrows remind me of my station in life here. "That phone's not going to answer itself," he says. He snatches the cordless from its cradle and slides it along the counter towards me like it's a glass of beer in an old Western saloon.

I pick up the phone and shoot a glance at Scott. He's the boss and I'm not. I tap the 'talk' button and cradle the cordless to my ear. "Cinematic, this is Guillermo. How can I help you?"

"What'd you say? Is this Cinematic?" It's a man's voice, loud and obnoxious. A woman's voice fills the background.

"That's what I just said, sir," I reply. "Any other questions?"

The guy on the line cups his phone speaker. Muffled yelling ensues. He's telling his female companion to shut up. Then he comes back on.

"Sorry about that. Can you check to see if I have an account there? I can't fucking remember," he says. "I'm in a rush."

I give a tiny sigh. "Can I get your name?" This guy's a store whore, you know the type. People who have so many memberships, they can't keep track of them all. How hard is that?

"It's Chris Donaldson," he says. "Might be under Christopher. And like I said, I'm in a hurry, so chop-chop, please."

I find his name on the membership list when it clicks in my head. He's Christopher Donaldson, big-time action director. His last two movies, Annihilator, and Annihilator 2 made over five hundred million combined at the box office, according to the trades. I never saw either of them, don't need to. He's just the latest Hollywood hack, albeit a rich one. But why him and not me? That's the mantra in this town.

"Christopher Donaldson," I tell him. "Yes sir, you're a member here." My manager Scott puts his magazine down on the counter and looks my way. *Now* he's interested in the call.

"About fucking time," Donaldson says. "I'm looking for some movies."

Now it's become a snoop call. Customers who can't, or won't search the titles for themselves. *Always get them in the store,* Scott tells us. *In the store and they'll buy more.*

I throw Donaldson a line to see if he bites. "We're open 'til ten if you'd like to come in and browse our selection," I tell him. "You might find some other movies to rent. We've also got some cool director t-shirts, film books, and popcorn."

"Don't need that other shit, I've got to be in the Valley in an hour," Donaldson says. "I need you to bring the movies to my car, if you've got them."

Scott's still looking at me, trying to eavesdrop on the conversation. "Sir, we can't do that for you," I tell Donaldson. "You're welcome to come in and take a look—"

"Do you fucking know who I am?" Donaldson screams into the receiver. "I need these movies for a ninety-million dollar pitch at Warner Brothers in an hour. Traffic is going to suck ass. Do I need to spell it out?"

I've met lots of cool movie people while working at the store. Donaldson isn't one of them. "I'm sorry sir," I tell him. "Here at Cinematic we serve all of our customers equally. That means no special

111

treatment."

There's silence on Donaldson's end of the line. Now Scott grows even more interested in my phone call. He scribbles something down on a yellow Post-It note and holds it up for me to read: WHAT DOES HE WANT???

"Listen, you shit stain," Donaldson bellows. "My last movie made more money than you'll make in a lifetime. You understand that? Now tell me—"

"Please hold," I tell Donaldson.

I punch the "hold" button and tell Scott what Donaldson wants. His eyes go wide and he tells me how we've got to help Donaldson out. How it would be bad for business if we piss him off. I let out a weary sigh and bite my tongue. This fucking town. I take Donaldson off hold.

"—you fucking got that?" Donaldson shouts from his end. "Now put your manager on the phone."

"Actually, I'm the manager, sir. My name is Guillermo," I say. I often pretend to be the manager with difficult customers, since Scott avoids conflict like the plague. "I can help you. What movies are you looking for and where are you parked?"

On Donaldson's end of the call there's more static and more yelling at his female companion. Then the sounds of rustling paper. "About damn time, Gandalf," Donaldson spits. "Here's my list: I need Eisenstein's Mexico movie, something called *I Am Cuba*, and *Touch of Evil* by Welles. You got those?"

"We do carry them, let me check if they're in the store and not rented out," I say. "Please hold."

Five minutes later I've got the movies in hand and I pick up the phone. "Sir, you're in luck, those are in."

Donaldson grumbles at his lady friend, then he's back on the line. "About fucking time," he says. "Charge them to my card, alright? I'm parked in the alley behind the store, it's the blue BMW 750i."

I throw the DVDs into a plastic "THANK YOU" bag and walk out the back door of the store. Donaldson's BMW is sitting there idling with the trunk popped open. He's squabbling with his girlfriend when he sees me and rolls down the window.

He tears the aviators off his face and glares at me. "Throw them in the trunk. And tell Geronimo he's an asshole. You got that?"

I put the videotapes in the trunk and thump it after closing. Without hesitating, Donaldson peels out, tires screeching. Tearing down the alley, he takes the corner on two wheels and disappears. Time for my lunch break.

‡

The following week, it's a busy Friday night when the cordless rings. A tickle forms in my stomach. Scott, in a surprising move, picks up the phone. After talking to the caller, he offers me the handset. "It's Donaldson, he's asking for you," Scott tells me. "Actually he asked for Gilbert, but I think he means you."

Figures. Assholes latch onto me like flies on shit. I roll my eyes and take the phone from Scott.

"Don't piss him off," Scott says. "We need the business." He stands closer to me so he can eavesdrop on the call.

I cradle the phone to my ear. "This is Guillermo, how can I help you?"

"Gabriel," Donaldson says. "Thanks for your help last week, you saved my ass. Of course, those pricks at the studio didn't like my idea, but fuck them. I need another favor from you."

My neck tenses up and my eyes go to Scott. He mouths the words "WHATEVER HE NEEDS" to me. I nod my head NO at Scott. I'm not going to put up with this jackass again. Scott mouths the words "DO IT FOR CINEMATIC." A beat later, I bite my tongue until I can taste the blood in my mouth.

"Hello? You still there?" Donaldson says.

I take a deep breath. "I'm here, Mr. Donaldson, what can I do for you?"

A yippy dog whines in Donaldson's background. He yells at someone. "Get this fucking dog out of here," he says to them. Then he's back. "Okay Gideon, here's what I need."

I cover the phone's receiver and let out a sigh. Scott is practically breathing down my neck, straining to hear the conversation.

On the phone, ice cubes clink inside a glass. A drink is poured. Donaldson takes a sip and exhales. "I want you to close the store," he says.

A frown grows on my face. "Why would I close the store, sir?" I tell him.

"Here's the deal," Donaldson says. "I'd like to come in and look for some movies to rent, but I don't want anyone else in there. How much does the store make in an hour? Whatever it is, I'll pay it."

My teeth hurt from grinding. "Please hold, sir."

Scott leans in, anxious to hear the latest demand. "What's he want now?"

I let out another long sigh. "He wants to close the whole fucking store for an hour so he can shop alone."

"This will work," Scott says, rubbing his hands together like Scrooge McDuck. "We're behind on rent and need the money. Tell him it'll cost two grand."

I give Scott a bullet-eyed stare. "I suppose you want me to work that night too."

"Could you?" Scott says with a pleading look. "Donaldson isn't going to want anybody else here. You know he likes you."

"Fine," I say. "Let's see what he says."

I pick up the phone and take it off hold. "Sir, we can accommodate you, it's going to cost you three thousand." Scott gives me a *no you didn't* look.

More dog whining on Donaldson's end of the call. "Three grand huh?" he says. "Popular spot. I'll give you twenty-five hundred."

"Deal," I tell him. "When would you like to come in?"

Donaldson yells at someone to get him another drink. "I'll be there in an hour," he says.

"An hour?"

He hangs up, dial tone filling my ears.

I look at Scott. "You want to make the announcement or should I?"

‡

An hour later at 10pm, I've locked the front door and and put up a sign that says CLOSED FOR PRIVATE EVENT. Disappointed customers try to talk their way inside to no avail. Scott's told the rest of the staff to go home. Still no sign of Donaldson. We're open until 11 on Fridays, but now this jackass is pushing his luck. Scott straps on his backpack and heads toward the back door. "Let me know when he shows up," he says. "I'll be home." Then he leaves.

By 11 o'clock, Donaldson still hasn't shown up. I've been watching *The Maltese Falcon* on the store TV while I wait. Such a great movie. More customers reach the front door, read the sign, and leave in a huff. Some drop off their movies in the return slot with a thud. At 11:15, I decide to call it a night. I've turned everything off and gathered my things when there's a loud pounding at the back door. Of course.

I grab the store's security system—an old Louisville Slugger—and slowly approach the back door. "We're closed," I say. "Who is it?"

"That you, Gideon?" says Donaldson. "My apologies, I was detained. Can we still do this?"

I open the back door and there he is, Mr. Bigshot Hollywood director. He's a lot shorter in real life. Most celebrities are, unless it's Liam Neeson or Conan O'Brien, those fuckers are tall, I've seen them in person. "I was about to close up," I tell him. "We didn't think you were going to show."

Donaldson struts in with his gal pal, a leggy blonde who's wearing too much perfume and a skirt that would fit better on a small child. "I'll only be half an hour, tops," he slurs. "Want to show me around?" His Glenfiddich breath mixes with his lady friend's Chanel No. 5 and makes my head swirl.

"Step right in," I say, shutting the door behind them.

Donaldson stumbles around the racks lined with VHS boxes and DVD cases. "You got an Italian horror section? I might be doing a Giallo picture next, whatever the hell that means."

I point him to the back corner of the store. "Right there. It's categorized by director—Argento, Fulci, Bava—"

Donaldson's girlfriend stops in the center of the store and checks her fingernails. "I'm bored," she announces. "How long we going to be here?"

Donaldson is busy looking at the giallo movie covers. "Not long, baby," he tells her. "Keep your panties on."

I drop my backpack on the floor next to the cash register when my stomach growls. I was going to grab some Taco Bell on the way home, but the drive-thru near my place closes at midnight. Donaldson is going to take his sweet time, that's for sure.

"Where do you keep the Westerns?" Donaldson says. His girlfriend hasn't moved from the spot she stopped on. She picks up a VHS box and studies it.

"They're around the corner here," I say, leading him to the Western section. "Grouped by director, of course. Any specific one you looking for?"

Donaldson's hands are full with VHS boxes he's picked up. "Have you got that one with Toshiro Mifune and Bronson? Red something?"

Wow. Donaldson actually has taste in movies? Quite surprising for a Hollywood hack. "*Red Sun*," I say. "Great movie. We do have it." I pick the movie off the shelf and hand it to him.

He trades me his stack of rental picks so that he can peruse the VHS box for Red Sun. "Fox wants me to direct a remake of this, but their script sucks. Figured I should check out the original."

"Why not just adapt a novel, baby," Donaldson's girlfriend says. "There are plenty of books that would make great movies. Why not make a movie of *The Notebook*? That one made me cry."

Donaldson turns to his lady friend. "Did I ask you to say something? Go read another book or something." Then he looks at me and rolls his eyes. He grabs another handful of VHS boxes from the Western section and hands them to me. "I'll take these too."

For the next hour, I escort Donaldson from section to section as he collects even more movies to watch. It's around midnight when I tell him I've got to eat something.

"Alright, I think that's it, Gerardo." We walk back to the register and Donaldson drops a pile of movie boxes onto the counter next to the ones I already put down for him. "Ring me up." His girlfriend dozes on Scott's stool behind the counter.

Altogether, I count forty-two movies for Donaldson. "Sir," I tell him, "Just so you know, these are all due back on Sunday by 10pm."

"Got it," Donaldson says. He turns to his girlfriend. "Hear that, honey? Daddy's got to watch all of these movies over the weekend."

She pouts. "You promised me a spa day at the Two Bunch Palms." Donaldson looks at me and shrugs. "I know darling, but this is work. You can go to Palm Springs without me," he tells her. "Kyle can take you there and then go shopping with you afterwards."

The girlfriend frowns. "I don't like Kyle, you know that."

Donaldson rolls his eyes at me.

"Your total comes to one hundred and fifty-nine dollars with tax," I say. Donaldson doesn't blink an eye and hands me his silver Amex card. Never seen one of those before. I swipe it and the sale comes back approved.

It takes six plastic shopping bags to fit all of his movie rentals. Donaldson grabs three bags with each hand and yells at his girlfriend. "Daphne, time to get back in the car. We're going home." She wakes with a startle.

I walk them to the back door and open it. "Thanks and have a good night," I tell them. "Enjoy the movies."

Donaldson looks at me. "Sure, Gustavo."

"It's Guillermo," I tell him. "You haven't gotten it right once."

"Okay then," he says. "Have a good one."

After I shut everything down and lock up, I head to my car. The Taco Bell over on Pico and Bundy is open 24 hours, there's still time to get some food.

‡

The following Wednesday, I'm restocking movies when the phone rings and I pick up. "Cinematic, this is Guillermo, how can I help you?" Instead of a response, there's just ragged breathing. It sounds like the caller's up to two packs of cigarettes a day, easy.

After a coughing fit that lasts for nearly a minute, the caller finally speaks. "Gordon, how you doing, it's Chris," he says. "Chris Donaldson."

This fucker hasn't gotten my name right once. "My name is Guillermo, I just said it."

"That's right," he says. "I got your manager's calls about the late tapes." More coughing. "I haven't been feeling well."

I shrug as if Donaldson can see me over the phone. "Sir, the movies you rented were due three days ago. We need those back. Those are the only copies we have."

"I know, I know," Donaldson says. "I've only watched half of them. Can't I just buy them from you?"

Now this jackass is acting like a tardy buyer—the kind of customer who would rather pay the full price for a VHS or DVD than the late fees incurred.

I pull the cordless away from my head like I want to throw it across the room. I bring it back to my face. "Here at Cinematic, we pride ourselves on stocking hard-to-find movies," I tell Donaldson. "They're irreplaceable sir, and not for sale. We're open until 10pm tonight if you'd like to return them. For every day you don't bring them back, you are incurring late fees. Sorry, but those are the rules."

Donaldson takes a long, wheezing breath. "I can't come in, I feel like shit." His voice sounds faint, like he's whispering from across a big empty room. "I need you to come to my place. I can give you the tapes back and cut you a check. How's that sound?"

Now this fucker wants me to drive out to god knows where to pick up the damn movies? "Sir," I say, "Don't you have an assistant who can do that for you?"

Donaldson sounds tired, defeated. "Daphne? She stayed in Palm Springs for the week. I live in the Palisades, it's not that far from you. I'll give you gas money for coming out, I swear."

"Hang on a minute," I tell him. I put the call on hold and find Scott, who's chatting up some blonde co-ed in the silent movie section. I fill him in on the situation.

"Sounds like he wants you to go pick up the movies," Scott says. "Is your car running okay? Want to take mine?"

Not the answer I wanted to hear. "Seriously?"

Scott steps away from the girl he's been talking to and leans into my ear. "I'll give you an extra night off next week. Your pick. But not Friday or Saturday night, you know how busy it gets those nights."

I give Scott the side-eye.

He checks his surroundings for other employees within earshot and leans in even closer to me. "Tuesdays are dead. Take next Tuesday off and I'll pay you for it anyway. Just don't tell anyone, alright?"

"Make it Tuesday and Wednesday night off," I tell Scott, unmoving.

He cocks his head at me like I'm crazy. "Alright, deal. Now get those tapes back."

I nod. "Will do. If I'm not back in an hour, call the cops," I say. "Seriously."

Back on the phone, Donaldson gives me his address and then I hang up. I head to my car and get in. Then I pull out onto Santa Monica Boulevard and head toward the Palisades.

‡

Donaldson's place is only six miles from the store, but it's a Saturday night and the traffic's at a standstill on Sunset. If you're going anywhere in LA, so are five hundred other people, it's a given. I check the street sign up ahead when I realize I missed a turn. I study the Thomas Guide sitting on the passenger seat for a quick sanity check. Square J-5. 1469 Albright Street. Yep, I should've taken the street behind me. I could walk to his place faster.

The next chance I get, I make a right and weave my way back to Albright. The street's lined with palm trees and looks like someplace out of Lifestyles of the Rich and Famous. I park at the mansion next to Donaldson's and get out of the car. As I walk up his driveway, I notice his place is more modest than the others on the block. Still nice, though.

I ring the doorbell. It's a quiet neighborhood, nice and clean, with space between the houses. Nothing like the cement city that's my neighborhood.

I press the doorbell again and hear footsteps approaching from inside. Then a voice. "I'm coming. That you Gilbert?" Donaldson says through the door.

"It's Guillermo, sir," I reply. This guy's never going to remember my name. Maybe that's a good thing.

The door opens. Donaldson's wearing just a terry cloth robe and flip-flops, a rocks glass in his hand.

"Welcome," he slurs. He waves me inside. "Please, come in. Mi casa es su casa."

I step into the foyer as he closes the door behind me. "Thanks," I say as I reach into my back pocket. "I've got your late fee total right here. You can make the check out to Cinematic and I'll get out of your hair. Have you got the movies?"

Donaldson turns and disappears into the house without saying a word. Ice cubes are dropped into a glass and a drink is poured.

I don't want to leave the foyer. "If you can just write the check, I'll be on my way," I call out. "And don't forget the movies."

Donaldson raises his voice from wherever he's gone to. "I bought this place after *Annihilator 2* made a shit-ton of money," he says. "The house was a steal at thirty million. You believe that shit?"

Now Donaldson's a money bragger—assholes who talk about how cheap their rent is or what a deal they got for some stupid high-dollar item. While I wait for him, I notice a sitting room on the right. There's an Eames chair and a Mondrian on the wall that have to be reproductions. Unless they're real. Again, Donaldson proves he's got taste.

"Sir," I speak up again. "Don't you want to see the total amount you owe?"

Donaldson reappears before me in the foyer with two drinks in hand. He offers me one of them. "I figured you for a vodka tonic man, am I right?"

After a silent beat, I realize we're the only ones in the house.

"No thanks, I really should get back to the store," I tell him. "Do you have the movies?"

He stares at me like a tiger locked onto a lone gazelle in some nature documentary.

My heart beats a little louder. "If you can just give me the movies, I'll get out of your hair, sir."

Donaldson finishes one of the drinks with a swallow and

sets down the glass. "You're a movie guy," he says. "How about a quick tour of the house?"

Now this asshole wants to show me his sex dungeon? No thanks. "I really need to get going," I tell him. "I just need those movies, you can mail us the check."

"Nonsense," Donaldson says as he wraps an arm around me. "The tour will only take a minute. Besides, there's something I want to show you."

He escorts me deeper into the house, past the sunken living room below us. Behind it, three large bay windows look out onto a patio and beyond that, the sloping hillside. Prime real estate.

"Nice view, right?" Donaldson says. "That's not even the best part." He takes a sip from the drink he offered me. "Check this out."

He opens a door, to reveal a darkened stairway beyond.

I hesitate but feel his arm nudging me gently toward the stairs. "The store was busy when I left, I should get back," I say.

He flips the light on for the stairs down. "Your boss doesn't give a shit. You want to work in a video store the rest of your life? C'mon."

Donaldson walks ahead of me down the stairs, his flip-flops slapping. This is the part where he shows me his S&M chamber and I get the fuck out of here, screw the damn movies.

At the foot of the stairs is a long hallway lined with two doors on each side.

"What's behind Door Number One?" he says as he opens the one closest to us. He flips on the light switch. It's a room bigger than my entire studio apartment in Mar Vista. Wooden boxes line the scores of shelves in the room. The air is smoky and sweet. "You like cigars?" he asks.

"I don't smoke," I tell him.

Donaldson pulls a cigar from one of the boxes and lights it up. "Suit yourself," he says. "More Cohibas for me. Let's move on."

Down the hallway, he opens the next door and turns on the light. Instead of carpet, the floor is covered with Astro-Turf. Sitting against the back wall is the biggest projection TV I've ever seen. A golf bag with a full set of clubs squats in front of the screen. "This is the game room," Donaldson says. "Right now, I'm working on my short game. Did you know Bentley made golf clubs?"

I nod 'no' and check my watch.

"Me neither," he says, pulling a nine-iron from the bag. "These fuckers cost a shitload, that's for sure." He ushers me out of the room with the club. "Now for the moment you've been waiting for."

We walk past another door and Donaldson points to it. "Not that one, that's the bathroom."

He opens the last door in the hallway and hits the light. My eyes go wide. The room is two stories high. Auditorium seating with three rows of leather recliners. A reflective screen that covers the entire back wall. Red velvet curtains adorn the sides. It's fucking amazing.

Donaldson grins at my reaction. "Sweet, huh? This is where I watch everything. I can screen film or video, whatever I want. Projection booth's upstairs."

"Holy shit," I say. "What did this cost?"

Donaldson wags his nine-iron at me. "I don't remember, but it was worth it. The same guy designed screening rooms for Spielberg and DePalma," he says. "He ain't cheap. And check this out." He motions to the wall closest to us. It's a large bookcase filled with movie props and other memorabilia. He grabs one and holds it up. "This is the stanchion gun from *Annihilator*."

Up close, the prop gun looks cheap and flimsy. "Cool," I say.

Donaldson senses my disappointment. "These things always look better on the big screen, right?"

I nod 'yes.'

He grabs another prop, a black statuette of a bird, and hands it to me.

"Now this, is the pièce de résistance," he says. "This is one of the original three they made for the film. You familiar with *The Maltese Falcon*? The John Huston picture?"

The bird's heavy in my hands. "Of course. What's it made of?" I say.

"Mostly plaster," he tells me. "See the difference between this and the stanchion gun? Those old Hollywood prop guys really knew how to make quality stuff. They were craftsmen."

Who knew Donaldson was such a purist?

He takes the black bird from me and puts it back on the shelf. "Just answer me a question, then I'll get your movies."

"Sure," I say. "But then I've really got to get going."

He leans in so close that I can smell the Grey Goose and Cohiba on his breath. "You really want to work in a video store your whole life?"

I slowly take a step back.

Donaldson points the nine-iron at me like an old-time school teacher. "You want to make movies, am I right? I can always tell the real ones from the posers," he says. "You remind me of myself when I was your age–hungry and willing."

My tongue's a dry sponge.

Donaldson unties the sash on his robe and it spills open. He's not wearing anything underneath. His stomach looks like a hairy bean bag about to burst, with his junk dangling below.

I struggle to avoid his stare and take another step back, my heart pounding. "Mr. Donaldson, you can keep the movies, I'll just show myself out."

"Don't go," he says. "Things are just getting interesting." He drops the lit cigar into his glass and it hisses, then goes dark.

I reach for the door handle behind me and turn it, but Donaldson pushes it shut with his nine-iron.

"How hungry and willing are you, Gerald?" he says. "You help me and I'll help you. That's how it works in Hollywood. Or didn't you know that?"

I scoot away from the door and along the bookcase filled with memorabilia. A glance around the room tells me there's no other way out of here.

Donaldson sets his glass aside. "Kid, you don't make it in this town without giving up a piece of yourself," he says. "You get me?"

I'm cornered. Nowhere else to go but the recliners. "Don't touch me," I tell him.

Donaldson grips his nine-iron with both hands like he's going to take a swing. "Now get down on your knees," he says.

I scramble over a recliner so that it's between us. "You're fucking crazy," I say.

Donaldson takes a practice swing. "You want to make movies? You've got to pay the price. No need to make it complicated."

"I don't want to know what you've done to get where you are," I say.

"I've done some nasty things, if that's what you mean," Donaldson says. "I paid my dues. And now it's your turn."

"Fuck you," I tell him. I make a run for the door.

Donaldson swats at me with the club, but misses.

I get to the door and fumble with the handle, his raspy breath behind me. A soft breeze caresses the side of my face for a moment, then a bone-shattering snap as Donaldson brings his nine-iron down on my left forearm. Searing white-hot pain fills my eyes as I collapse to the floor in a heap. This fucker's broken my arm. I groan like a hungry baby.

Donaldson towers over me. He lets his robe fall down to his feet. His pecker's standing at full attention now. "Don't make me hit you again. You need one good arm to do what I like."

I manage to scoot away from him along the bookcase, favoring my left arm. The room spins a little and my stomach twists. I'm going into shock.

"You newbies are all the same," Donaldson says. "It's not talent that gets you ahead. It's willingness. How much have you got?"

I shuffle backward some more, my left arm is swollen now and burns like hell. It might only be a fracture and not a break. I'm not sure which one I'd prefer right now.

Donaldson takes a swing at the bookcase for dramatic effect, smashing several movie props in the process. "Now what's it going to be?" he says. "I don't want to smash in that pretty little face of yours."

My back up against the bookcase, I manage to get up on my feet. My left arm's on fire and my eyes are filled with stabbing white flashes. With my right hand, I feel around behind me for something I can use as a weapon.

Donaldson frowns. "I didn't tell you to stand up."

The fingers of my right hand wrap around something solid. Sculpted feathers on it. A beak.

"Fuck off," I say, swinging my right arm around.

The black bird statuette hits Donaldson square in the jaw. The impact makes him lose his balance and fall backward. On the way down, his head catches the back of a recliner and his neck lurches forward with a nasty crunch like a celery stick being snapped in half. Donaldson slumps to the floor in a dead heap.

My eyes go wide.

I crawl over to Donaldson. He stares at the ceiling above as if he's watching the movie of his life play out. He's conscious, but he isn't breathing. My left arm is swollen and puffy, so with my right arm, I take his hand and hold it tight. His muscles have gone slack. He pisses himself. In a blink he's gone, his eyes frozen. No one deserves to die like this, not even Donaldson. I stumble to a phone and dial 9-1-1.

‡

A week later, I'm back at Cinematic, restocking movies with my good arm. Since the incident, the store's been busy. Scott even tells me he's going to promote me to assistant manager. We'll see if that really happens.

Most of the people who come into the store just want to know what happened with Donaldson. Some want to sign my arm cast. A few of them are even famous faces you might recognize. Before I can give them the gory details though, Scott always interrupts and tells them to go read the *Times* story if they're that interested.

Donaldson's even gotten his own endcap at Cinematic, an honor only bestowed upon a select group of filmmakers. It was Scott's idea. They're always rented out, which is fine. I'm not interested in seeing his filmography.

Although I thought he was a talentless hack, Donaldson was right about one thing. I don't want to work in this place forever. In the meantime, the muse has kissed me full on the lips and I can't push her away. I've got an idea for the Great American Screenplay everyone's going to be talking about. It's the sad story of a nutball Hollywood director gone mad. It might just rank up there with *Citizen Kane*.

Victor De Anda is a writer in Philadelphia who enjoys watching movies and searching for good Mexican food. His fiction has been published in Mystery Tribune, Shotgun Honey, Pulp Modern Flash, and Punk Noir Magazine, with more forthcoming. He is on Twitter @victordeanda.

Mouthfeel

Robert P. Ottone

"There's a lot of heat up front," David said, sipping from his usual burgundy glass.

"Right? That's what I thought, too. It's like the barrel's on fire or something. I'm not really getting it," Ava said, wiping the sweat from her brow and tying her blond locks into a messy bun. "It shouldn't taste like fire. It should be earthy, sure, but not *scorched* earth."

"These were new barrels?" he asked, staring at the rows of oak containers, all of them the same vintage, all of them, presumably, tasting like a campfire that refused to die.

Ava nodded. "Got them off the truck myself. Nothing's changed. I've checked the grapes. I've checked the damn soil. I've checked our suppliers. I've checked the minerality. I've checked every single thing. Nothing is out of the ordinary."

"And yet … unpleasant." David said, taking another sip. He furrowed his brow. "This was supposed to be a flagship for us this year. Not good for your first batch as head vintner."

Ava sat down on one of the sealed barrels and sighed, wiping sweat from her brow. So much time spent preparing, testing, making adjustments, working on other vintages, and here, her pet project, shot to hell. All that time down the drain, almost literally. All of October so far had been spent knee-deep in dirt checking minerality and acid levels of the soil. Just a bad batch, she came back to, over and over.

When Ava got hired at the vineyard in Sonoma, she was all-too-ecstatic. She knew every nuance of the vineyard's 2011 award-winning cab-sav, and found herself emulating it the best she could, using the same heritage of grape, grown in the same soil, the same minerality. She found inspiration in the vineyard's history, the family's journey from Europe to America, steeped in liquid tradition, finding herself drawn to their product long before she worked for the winery.

She had always felt drawn to the west coast, and when an opportunity arose at the vineyard she had her heart set on, the one that inspired her beyond all others, she thought she'd make a splash. She didn't think that splash would be for making the worst wine in the vineyard's history. This was where she *needed* to be. The west coast was *everything*. Her parents never understood why. Her friends didn't, either. But they all knew that somehow, Ava would end up there. The opportunity at the winery was perfect.

"You've gotta' make it work, Ava," David said, finally, wiping his glass clean and grimacing at the taste still lingering in his mouth and tossing what was left into a nearby bucket. "We stole you away from those Hudson Valley upstarts for a reason. You need to make good."

She nodded. Arguing would be futile. Instead, she ran through her available options. *Additives? More oxygen? Lemon?* The usual go-tos wouldn't help. She'd added enough oxygen that if she fired the wine into space, it'd be able to breathe on its own for a week and a half.

"I will, David. I swear," she said, looking up at her boss.

"You better," he said, handing her the glass. He smoothed his navy blazer, turned on his heels, and walked out of the lab, converted from an old barn on the vineyard's massive property.

Ava filled the glass, poured herself some of the wine and took a sip. Instantly, the taste of scorched earth flooded her mouth, and the feeling of ash washed over her tongue, a delicate balance between the vulgar notes of soot and coal.

‡

Ava sat in the hay loft above the barn. There was some spare equipment, but other than that, it was bare. She felt alone. Sometimes, it was the only place she could go at the vineyard that let her really drift with her thoughts. Other times, she felt a kind-of presence with her.

It was impossible for Ava to articulate really, and she wasn't one for superstition, but she'd heard rumors of haunted vineyards ever since she started working in the industry. These stories made for good marketing come Halloween, usually the end of the season on the east coast, but here in Sonoma, it didn't add much to the vineyard's business.

The faintest whiff of a campfire drifted in the air, and Ava breathed in deep. It wasn't unlike the scorched taste of the wine. But there was more to it. Lavender notes, floral in a way Ava hadn't picked up previously.

Like perfume.

‡

That night, Ava walked among the rows of grapes, looking for a reason the wine lost its sense of self for the hundredth time that week. For all intents and purposes, the wine should be a robust bouquet of black pepper, orange zest, and plum. The grapes had been used for ages, the same vines, the same rows.

As she walked the trellises, her mind continued to race. *My job is at stake, you jerks,* she thought, directing her anger at the inanimate fruit who held her future in the industry within their apparently-corrupted flesh. The aroma of the grapes was intoxicating and something Ava always loved about working at the winery.

There was comfort here. Familiarity. She'd never felt it at any of the other vineyards she'd worked at before, but here, nestled in Sonoma, it was like she was home.

Sometimes she'd lay under the vines, breathing in the dirt of the land and the fruit of the vine and try to center herself. She believed it was what made her a great winemaker. There was an intimacy between her and the grape. Between her and the juice.

"This is crazy," she finally said. "Just a bad batch. Nothing more."

The lights strung above the vineyard cast a soft yellow glow over the trellises, providing enough visibility for walking, with just enough shadow to let imagination dance wildly. She spent many nights walking the rows, a cool California breeze tousling her wild, curly blond locks.

Just a bad batch …

Ava froze, hearing her words repeated back to her.

"Hello?"

Only the rustling of leaves. She remained silent in the vineyard, holding her breath, half-expecting one of her coworkers to hop out and scare her, but nothing came. She looked down the rows and between the clusters of vines for the source of the voice but couldn't find one.

‡

For another week, Ava did her best to work on the barrels. She slaved over them, trying new things, looking up new strategies online, calling her friends at other vineyards and running through all of their proposed ideas. Nothing worked.

In the dark, working tirelessly on the vines, Ava was possessed by the idea of something watching her from the foliage. Something seen briefly on the periphery of her vision, only to vanish entirely when she'd turn her head toward it. A white-gray blur. The faint aroma of a distant fire pit.

Putting in so many late nights, Ava believed she was overworked. Overtired. That maybe she was losing her mind.

Until she saw her. A woman in a soft, light dress, standing barefoot among the vines. The first time Ava got a good look, she thought she was dreaming. That her exhaustion had taken its toll and she'd finally been broken by the heady aroma of grape, extract and flavors lingering in her work area.

Then the woman returned. Night after night. Always about fifty feet from the open converted barn. Always watching. Silent. As if waiting.

She didn't understand the woman's fascination. Every time she'd approach her, she'd somehow disappear, whether behind a delivery truck, into the vineyard itself, or behind the barn.

Sometimes, when Ava left in the evening, she'd wave to the woman, who she thought might be with the cleaning crew, but she never so much as waved back and instead only stared.

‡

One morning, Ava ran through a variety of resources to potentially right the barrels of borderline-toxic, undrinkable wine. Sweeteners, both natural and unnatural didn't work, the taste of ash and soot refused to die.

By lunch time, she found herself in the vineyard again, sitting on a blanket, eating a sandwich, and thinking. Her favorite way to unwind during the day was to take lunch among the rows of grapes, breathing the air they breathed, and grounding herself in the soil they were grounded in. She sipped the bad batch and sighed to herself.

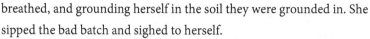

There was loneliness. Being on the west coast meant leaving her friends and family, but that loneliness was usually chased away by her work. With her work not coming together, the loneliness was overwhelming.

"Why so glum, girly?"

Ava looked up and was blinded by the sun for a moment. As her eyes adjusted, she could make out a young woman with hair that reminded Ava of the autumn leaves back in upstate New York, the halfway blend of red and orange and altogether vibrant.

Ava reached her hand up to block the sun to better see the woman. Young, lovely, pale. "Sorry, sun got in my eyes a sec."

"I can see that," the woman said, looking around at the rows of grapes. There was a faint hint of an accent. *Irish? Scottish?*

"I'm sorry, did you get separated from a tour or something? Can I help you?"

"Your memory ain't what it used t'be, I see."

There was something remarkably familiar about her. Ava was amazed at the wave of comfort that ran through her body when the redhead stepped closer.

"Nah, I don't need much help," she said after a moment, looking around, running her fingers along the vines. "I know m'way around this place, I think."

Ava nodded. "Who are you again?"

"Una."

"Hello, Una. I'm Ava."

"Yeah, I know. What're you doing out here by yerself? Don't the others think yer daft for being out here alone?"

Ava stared at the woman. "I don't really know what the others think. I'm new-ish. I'm just eating lunch."

Una stepped closer and sat down opposite Ava. She smoothed her vintage mint green lace dress and sat cross-legged, mimicking Ava. "What's fer lunch?"

Ava looked at her sandwich. "Bologna and cheese."

Una's eyes went wide, and she licked her lips. "M'favorite."

Their eyes locked and for a moment, Ava thought she saw a tiny flicker of orange light in the deep green of Una's iris.

"I'm sorry, I'm confused. Is there something I can do for you?"

Una reached out and grabbed the sandwich from Ava. "Maybe."

Una's mouth seemed to open impossibly wide, her jaw stretching with a click-clack of bone shifting against bone, and the sandwich disappeared quickly down her gullet, the strange girl barely taking a moment to savor the homemade pickles or avocado mayo Ava whipped up two nights earlier.

The great black maw of her mouth slowly closed, her plump red lips pursed then she sat, motionless. There was no chewing. Hell, Ava didn't even notice if she swallowed.

The redhead's face softened, and her eyes became expressionless and limp. For what seemed like an hour, but was only a matter of minutes, she stared at the vines, leaving Ava in shocked silence at the entire ordeal.

She could feel her heart racing and couldn't shake the image of Una's unhinged jaw from her mind.

"Una?"

Eventually, Una shook the cobwebs loose, and all life returned to her face. Her expression shifted from slack and dull to alive in a matter of seconds. "Yeah, that wasn't what I'm lookin' fer."

With that, Una rose and walked off, down the row of trellises, away from Ava.

Looking down at the hand that once held her well-prepared sandwich, Ava simply looked around confused and wondered, *what the hell just happened?*

‡

Back in the converted barn, Ava poured over the results of a new test to salvage the barrels. By blending pomegranate and raspberry juices with the juice of a blackened habanero, she hoped to mask the ashy, charcoal flavor that resided in the wine.

One slosh of the wine around her mouth indicated that her efforts were futile.

"Any luck?" David asked. He had been watching from the open barn doors, the light fading behind him, sky burning purple.

Ava shook her head. "Of course not. No change at all. I don't understand this. Everything about this wine is off. We should be getting notes of chocolate, pepper, orange. Instead, it's like licking the bottom of a God-damn ashtray."

David nodded. He inspected the wine, and noted the distinct, deep red color. "The thing is, it looks like a damn fine wine. Look at the cascade on the glass. It's damn near perfect."

Sighing, Ava looked over her lab setup. It wasn't much more than some beakers, burners, and a slew of ingredients, extracts, spices and more, but she could whip up magic when she needed to. None of her usual tricks were enough.

"I'll leave you to it," David said, starting out the door.

"Wait, David, who was that redhead that was here today? She with a tour or something? The cleaning crew? I've been seeing her around, late at night, I think. Irish accent or something?"

David froze in place. "Say that again?"

Ava furrowed her brow. "Sorry, yeah, I guess she's with the cleaning crew, but I was curious if you knew her. Name's Una."

He stepped closer. Ava couldn't tell if it was confusion or concern that washed over his face, and she worried a moment that this was the end. Her career was over. Her west coast adventure wrapping up all-too-early. David reached over and grabbed Ava's hand. "Come with me."

‡

As David led Ava into the winery's tasting room and up the stairs to his office, all Ava could think was that she was about to be fired. Talking to this Una person would get her shitcanned, and truth be told, Ava wasn't ready to go back to upstate New York. She wasn't ready to beg for her old job back, to explain to her family and friends how her big, exciting, life-changing move to California hadn't worked out.
She braced herself for the worst.

David pulled out a chair opposite his desk, and Ava sat down, preparing for the inevitable. "Listen, David, I'm sorry. I wasn't distracted, I promise. I was taking my lunch outside and—"

"Is this her?" David held out an old stack of photos, all of them laminated, but the photos themselves were ancient and yellowed. Many of them looked like they were made of metal, which Ava knew was the style of photography at the time.

Una stood among multiple figures who could easily be brothers, sisters, parents, grandparents. The left corner of her lip upturned in a sly grin, and wore the same mint green dress.

Ava nodded. "What are these, promo photos?"

David's eyes went wide, and he placed the photos out across his desk.

"You're sure this is who you saw?"

"Yeah, why?"

He sighed. "Ava, if who you saw is the same Una from these photos, then we may have bigger problems than just a bad batch of wine."

"Why?"

"Because these pictures are nearly two-hundred years old."

Ava stared at them. Slowly, it dawned on her what David was saying. After a moment, she leaned back in the leather chair and, without blinking, stammered to find the right response. "How is that possible?" is all she could muster.

"Folks see her," David said. "I never have, personally. Always thought it was bullshit, but every now and again, someone would see her hanging around. Sometimes near your barn. Sometimes near the tree at the center of the vineyard." He opened a small folder of photos. "This is from the rebuilding of the barn. The first one burned. The woman you keep seeing. The 'ghost,' well … she burned the place down after a horrible accident. Some kind of accidental hanging in the barn. I don't really know all the details."

Ava stared at the photos. Burnt rubble where her barn now stood. The reconstruction of the barn itself, in stages through various photographs.

"Tastes like fire …" Ava muttered to herself.

"What's that?" David asked.

"You never thought to tell me the place is haunted?"

"Is it, though? Anything bad happen?" David asked. "So far, the only bad thing that's happened to you is that your ability to make quality juice has seemingly vanished. Ghost or no ghost, that's the only real issue here."

David's words stung. Ava sighed and nodded, head hanging low. He wasn't wrong, as mean as he sounded. "Sorry."

David sighed. "I'm only hard on you because I know how great you can be. You know that, right?"

She nodded. "Yes sir."

‡

Hours later, sweaty and tired, Ava stood, examining glasses of the wine, searching deeply, glasses balanced at the end of her nose, hoping to find any indicator that would help tell her why the wine wasn't working.

First, her job was at risk, and now, she was being haunted by the daughter of the vineyard's founders from centuries earlier. Things simply were not looking up.

Ava rationalized that she was just going insane. Surely, losing one's mind is preferable to being haunted by the ghost of the Irish immigrant who built the very plantation you work for, right?

"Is that it? The wine that's giving you so much trouble?"

Turning, Ava saw that it was Una. Icy fingers ran down her spine as the pale spectre stepped into the barn, looking at the lights, the equipment, and large barrels of wine in neat rows along the massive walls.

"This place has changed a lot."

"I've only been here a little while, so, I don't really know," Ava said, her voice low. "New since you've been … umm … *alive*, I guess."

Una ran her fingers along the barrels. Her skin was porcelain, veins visible just under the flesh. In the sunshine, this was difficult to note, but in the dim light inside the barn, Ava made note of the woman's looks. She still wore the mint-colored lace dress and walked, carefully, toward Ava. Una was the Kodachrome vision of the photo, come to life.

"I know who you are," Ava said, slowly.

"Is that right?"

Ava nodded. "You're Una, the founder's daughter."

Una smiled. "And what else am I?"

"A ghost."

The redhead nodded. "I guess I am, huh? Sometimes we don't know that's what we are. That's why we walk around, doing the same things we did when we were alive. I know that I'm dead, o'course. I know *how* I died, *when* I died, all of it."

"I'm sorry …" Ava began.

Una stopped in her tracks. "Why, doll?"

"I just am. I don't know. I'm scared."

"Think I'm gonna' hurt ya'?"

Ava shrugged. "I don't know …"

"You say that a lot."

"I'm talking to a dead person, so, sorry I'm not super-conscious of what I'm saying."

Una laughed. A light wind blew into the barn. "What if I told you I came to help?"

Ava stared. Una walked around the room, tracing her slender, light fingers along the rows of barrels. For the first time, Ava noticed the girl's feet never touched the ground.

"Let me try it," Una said, grabbing a glass off a nearby rack and holding it out to Ava, rocking on her heels and smiling wide.

"Trust me, you don't want to, it's brutal," she said, shaking her head, remembering the horror of Una's lunchtime endeavors. Not seeing the deep, cavernous mouth that seemed to stretch on forever would be fine by Ava.

"I've had worse things, believe me," Una said with a smile. She's a tricky one, Ava thought. Up close, Una was lovely. Pursed red lips and that corner-smile that seemed to draw Ava in. There was a niggling suspicion that Ava had seen her before. The fleeting feeling of fingers entwined. The warmth of a body pressed against her own. Hours spent in the barn's hay loft, lips she could taste dancing against her own.

But that mouth … a shudder ran down Ava's back as she remembered the sound of Una's jaw crick-cracking open earlier.

Slowly, Ava poured a sample amount of wine in Una's glass. The ghost rolled the stem of the glass between her thumb and forefinger, letting the deep red wine glide along lazily. *She's done this before*, Ava smiled to herself.

"Slàinte mhath," Una said softly, raising the glass to her lips. She sloshed the wine around in her mouth a moment, and her eyes went completely black.

Una stood, frozen, her expression locked and eyes vacant of color and light. The bulbs in the barn flickered, and suddenly, Una was beside Ava, leaning against the lab station. Glass vials rattled and a bottle of cedar extract, which spilled to the ground, cracking open. The barn slowly filled with the aroma of cedar, light at first and then … *smoky*.

Shaking, Ava caught her breath and stared into the inky abyss where a pair of eyes should be.

Una's eyes dilated, the blackness fading and returning to their dark green color, the way cream blends with coffee; the shift in color was smokey and beautiful, altogether beguiling.

"Better?"

Ava nodded.

"You were right about the wine."

"I know."

"I know what it is, o'course."

Ava stared at her. "Tell me."

"Wouldn't be much fun in that. You gotta *earn* it, Ava."

"How?"

"With yer' heart and soul."

"Please, my job is on the line," Ava begged.

"How badly do you want to be here, in this place?"

"I belong here. I refuse to be fired and return home a failure."

Una leaned in close to Ava and looked down the nape of her neck.

"How did you find out that I'm a bogle?"

"A what?"

"A bogle. Sometimes we're called spirits, ghosts, whatever. I prefer the old country word. A *bogle.*"

"I saw your picture. In my boss' office."

Una nodded. "I've been watching you. Since you started."

Ava shook. There was an intense cold radiating off Una's body. "I saw you a few times."

"Because I *wanted* you to. Do you know how I died?"

"David didn't say." She could feel her arms shaking, her chest filling with heat. This was a fight or flight response and yet, her legs were rooted in place.

Una nodded. She leaned in close to Ava's ear. "Let me show you …"

The technology, barrels, and lab around Ava and Una melted away, and night turned into day. Una kept her icy hand clenched in Ava's as the barn began to look newer, more recent.

In place of the modern equipment and rows of barrels, the barn instead held farming equipment, hay bales, and wooden crates.

Without warning, Una, alive and in the flesh, ran into the barn. She was wearing the same dress she was wearing as a ghost-bogle-*whatever*, but here, her flesh was rosy and pink. She was truly alive.

She leaned against a hay bale and waited, nervously picking at her nails and smoothing her dress over and over, even though she looked lovely. A moment later, a young blond girl, who bore more than a passing resemblance to Ava, entered the barn, wearing overalls and a work shirt. It was clear she worked for the farm, which was in the early process of being converted into what would be the vineyard.

"Sorry to keep you waiting," the woman said, her voice low.

Una's face lit up, and in seconds, the two were in each other's arms, lips dancing together. They fell to the ground giggling, and passionately kissed atop a mound of hay.

"You're worth waitin' for, girly," Una said, kissing her with fervor.

Ava felt Una's grip tighten as the two watched the sweet expression of love unfold before them. Ava's heart quickened. In an instant, she was reminded of first love. The excitement. The thrill. It was Una's love. Una all along. She was there even when she wasn't. In Ava's own first kiss. Her own awkward fumblings with boys in the back seats of cars, in reality, it was always Una, inside her. Calling to her from Sonoma.

Suddenly, Una's expression changed. The two girls on the floor looked up, and standing in the doorway of the barn was Una's father, face red with anger.

He grabbed the blond girl and dragged her from Una's clutches.

Again, Una's grip tightened in Ava's and for a moment, she watched a tear fall from Una's gaze as the scene unfolded before them.

The world melted around them again, and now, in the barn, Ava and Una stood. It was night. Still the past. Ava looked around, confused. Fire blazed around them, the heat not unlike the taste of the bad batches Ava had been making. Heat. Wood. Hay. *Pure fire.*

"Where are we now?"

Una sighed. "Two nights later."

Ava continued looking around but could find no sign of the living Una or the young blond girl she loved. As Ava looked around the barn, a pair of legs suddenly dropped into her face. Screaming, she looked up, and spotted Una's hanged body, dangling from the hay loft.

She kicked for a moment, and then, slowly, all life faded from the girl's twitching body, her jaw going slack, stretching wide with the *clack-clack-clack* of her shattered jaw.

‡

With a flash of golden brilliance, Ava and Una were back in the modern barn. Ava struggled to catch her breath and wiped tears from her eyes.

"I'm so sorry, Una ..."

"All this time. Here. Waiting."

For a brief second, Ava remembered the call of the west coast. It was beyond a simple job offer. There was something before that. Something that she felt even as a young woman, in college, earlier, calling her west. New York was her home, but her soul, her entire being, she felt belonged on the west coast.

Ava looked up at the specter. "Waiting for me?"

Una nodded. "And now you're here."

Memories flooded Ava's mind. Remembrances that didn't belong to her. Things that she could never know. Ancient materials, dancing in and out of the darkness of her mind. It was as if she was remembering a song from childhood, once forgotten, every note and chord suddenly returning to her.

Ava spent a Christmas morning walking the winery, holding an unrecognizable yet familiar older man's hand.

She swung on a rope swing under the large canopy of an oak tree.

She held hands with the winery owner's daughter. Stealing kisses in the shade of trees, behind locked pantry doors, in musty, humid cellars.

She remembered how much she loved Una.

And she remembered how much Una loved her.

In an instant, Ava's lips met with the spirit's.

Their bodies entwined, and they fell to the floor of the barn, not far from where they fell centuries earlier. Ava felt her body begin to soften, as though she was melting into Una as they kissed.

It's alright. I promise it's alright.

"What's happening?"

You'll see...

A great, blinding light beamed from the barrels of wine in the barn. Ava's being trembled in the glow. Warmth, with faint hints of blackberry lingered on her tongue. On the back end of the kiss, there was heat.

They almost seemed to glow in the darkness as Una and Ava continued their coalescence.

‡

The following morning, David arrived to check on Ava's progress. In the barn, he found the same barrels of wine, but noted a distinct scent of citrus in the air. He poured himself a glass and sipped. Sloshing the liquid around his mouth, instead of spitting it out, he swallowed.

"Ava, where are you? You mad scientist, you did it!"

He looked all over the barn for Ava but came up empty.

In the hay loft above, Ava and Una sat, holding hands, watching the scene unfold below. Ava smiled.

The hay loft that would always be Ava and Una's.

Robert P. Ottone is the Bram Stoker Award-winning author of *The Triangle*. His other works include *Her Infernal Name & Other Nightmares* (an honorable mention in *The Best Horror of the Year Volume 13*) as well as suburban folk horror novel, *The Vile Thing We Created*. His short stories have appeared in various anthologies as well as online. He's also the publisher and owner of Spooky House Press. He can be found online at SpookyHousePress.com or on Twitter/IG: @RobertOttone. He delights in the creepy and views bagels solely as a cream cheese delivery device.

CAPTAIN OOZE

James Hadley Griffin

The summer the kids went missing, the Great Lakes rose to record levels. No one, not even the Harvard-degreed oceanographers and IPCC-certified climatologists, could explain why they were rising so dramatically — that June they had risen four inches higher than the record height in 1883. There was a lot of talk of the cyclical nature of the rising and falling of large bodies of water, the melting Canadian glaciers, the unusually high rainfall of the past decade.

But nothing provided a clear picture, nothing eased anyone's mind that this was a temporary anomaly and things would return to normal soon, though everyone sensed that something new and perhaps permanent was happening.

Melissa Yancey (aged nine and three-quarters, fair-skinned, with long red hair and freckles) could vaguely remember playing at the shore when she was three (sufficiently coated in SPF 50). She recalled the vast beach spreading far in front of her and easing elegantly into the teal-colored summer waters of Lake Michigan. And now, six years later and ten inches higher, the rising lake had reduced the beach to a shabby narrow strip between the lapping water and the swiftly eroding dunes. Strange things had started appearing in the water, formerly hidden by the dunes, including the bones of a schooner — the Blue Anglia — that had sunk in a storm in 1892. The dunes were beginning to regurgitate the past, as if a large, unseen wheel that had been turning for years was finally clicking back to where it had started, and old things that had gone away were returning.

Homeowners near the water were panicking and putting their houses on the market, the edges of their property cascading away into the lake, a little more every day. There were no buyers. Tourists stayed away, stayed home, went elsewhere. Campgrounds and RV parks were half-filled, if that.

And then the kids started disappearing.

Melissa's father Walt owned Yancey's Grill, a restaurant situated on a small sandy bluff above the Watenaw River, two miles from the lake shore. The grill was popular for its whitefish and trout dishes and Walt himself was a fixture in the town — with his salt-and-pepper walrus mustache, round black glasses and shiny bald head — he loved to wander from table to table on busy nights and chat it up with tourists and regulars alike. Usually, in the summer on such nights, Melissa hung out in the kitchen and helped with small chores like stacking dishes, peeling carrots or fetching frozen vegetables from the freezer for Carl, the head chef.

But this year, there were few nights when the restaurant was even more than half full and more often than not, Melissa grew bored sitting in Walt's office, the games and books she had brought having grown familiar and dull.

One night, in early June, only two weeks out from her last day of fourth grade, she idly sat on the floor of her dad's office. An hour before, she had just finished wiping down the menus and stacking them, then she counted and re-counted all the cans of stewed tomatoes. Now, with nothing else to do, she asked her dad if she could play outside. Walt told her to remain close to the restaurant and to come back in one hour. And absolutely, positively do not to go near the river.

"Right-er-roo, Daddy!"

He smiled. *Right-er-roo.* Where had she picked up that phrase?

Behind the grill was a small yard that led to a steep, ten foot sand bank which fell down to the clear, swift-moving water of the river.

For half an hour, amidst the clouds of small bugs bobbing across the top of the high grass, she played in the yard, mostly content with chasing her shadow and climbing the oak tree that grew near the southwest corner of the restaurant. But soon this too grew tiresome and, in spite of her dad's command, she decided to go explore down at the riverbank.

At the edge, she looked down. The record high water of the river had ripped into the bank below her feet and she noticed that, out of the sandbank, something had appeared, having been hidden for unknown years. It stuck out a few feet above the water at the sharpest bend in the river.

Squinting, she made out that it was the corner of a sign with the word "Captain" legible. She hesitated, and then jumped down onto the bank, feet sinking into the dense, wet sand, and made her way over to it. When she reached it, she dug her feet in and wiped away from the exposed corner a thin layer of sediment.

It was a drawing of a man with gaunt sunken features and round bulging eyes, sallow shiny skin, a high forehead with thin scraggly dark hair pulled back into a ponytail. He wore a dark tattered coat with heavy

brass buttons and fraying pants. One of his legs was a wooden peg. Below him was written a name: Captain Ooze. Cleary, he was styled to be some kind of pirate, but, for Melissa, the cartoonish nature of the drawing only rendered him more frightening and otherworldly. The ugliness of this figure burrowed into her mind in the way nursery rhymes or the rules of a simple game do. She had never had a notion of evil before, certainly not what "evil" looked like. She had seen pictures of "The Devil" with his red skin, pitchfork and horns but he never scared her because he seemed an impossible creature, unconnected to the real world. But Captain Ooze seemed like someone she might, or perhaps had, seen on the street, in the grocery store, at her dad's restaurant...

"Melissa!" She heard her dad's voice coming from the direction of the restaurant.

Melissa was startled out of her stupor, realizing that darkness had begun to fall. How long had she been standing there?

"Melissa! Where are you!"

"Here!" she yelled back.

She looked up and moments later her dad's head appeared over the top of the bank, his cheeks red.

"Get up here this instant!" he yelled.

She bit down on her lip, knowing she was in trouble, and scrambled up the bank to him. As they walked back together toward the restaurant he reprimanded her for disobeying him. She nodded her head, said she was sorry, that it would never happen again, but all the while she fixated on the image of Captain Ooze and that night, while she slept, he showed up again, as if he had climbed up off the sign and stowed away in her brain.

She was a heavy sleeper and an active dreamer. That night she dreamed of an unfamiliar backyard behind a tidy two-story red brick house. In the middle was a large birch tree from which hung a tire swing. On the swing was a boy from her class named Hollis Terry. They were casual friends from school and she tried to call out to him, but she discovered she had no voice and he couldn't see her. He pumped his legs, propelling himself higher and higher.

She turned and, from around the corner of the building, saw Captain Ooze come horribly to life, scarecrow tall with drooping arms poking from his coat and long fingers that nearly scraped the ground. His crooked skeleton bent him at hideous angles. Hollis, unaware, continued blissfully urging the swing upward.

Thud, thud, thud. The peg-legged Captain Ooze hobbled closer.

Melissa, in her dreams, tried to yell to Hollis to run, but she her voice felt trapped in her throat. Soon, the ghastly figure of Captain Ooze lurched and was upon Hollis. He quickly wrapped his hand around the boy's mouth, pulled him off the swing and, with an arachnidian gait, vanished into the woods that lined the far edge of the yard.

She awakened into the darkness of her room, her heart beating, a fearful, rasping squeak coming from her throat. She lay awake the rest of the night, staring into the darkness of her room, reminding herself over and over that nightmares aren't real.

The next evening, while Melissa helped roll silverware, she overheard her father getting a call in his office and she heard him speak the name: Hollis Terry. No, she heard him say, he hasn't seen the boy, and yes he will ask his daughter the same. Walt walked over to Melissa who trembled while she waited.

"Hey, Lissy. I got a quick question. Do you know a boy named Hollis Terry?"

She nodded. "He…he's in my class."

Walt noted her demeanor and continued. "Have you by chance seen him today or know where he might be?"

She shook her head. "No, sir."

He sat down next to her, took the silverware from her quaking hands and set it down. "The thing is…his parents don't know where he is. They're looking for him and need help finding him. If you know something, honey, you need to tell me."

She wanted to unburden herself to her father, to tell him about her dream and Captain Ooze, but she also wanted to feel like a big girl. Even though her counselor, Dr. Bryant, had told her it was okay to be scared, she knew that being afraid of things like dreams or monsters was for little kids.

"I don't know anything. I just hope he's okay."

Walt squinted at her.

"Well, darling, please tell me if you know or hear anything."

"I will, Daddy," she said, and went back to rolling the silverware.

That evening she overheard a mention of an Amber Alert on the news. Hollis was missing, last seen playing in his back yard.

Days passed with no sign of Hollis. His disappearance was all anyone talked about. She stayed with a neighbor while her father participated in a search party that combed the miles of dunes at the state park just north of town. No sign of him was discovered. No suspects were ever revealed. He had just blinked out of existence.

A week after Hollis's disappearance, Melissa had the second dream. She was in an unfamiliar house. It was shabby, with stained carpets, stacks of dishes in the sink, and bags of garbage piled by the back door. Two adults were quarreling loudly in the kitchen. Melissa couldn't understand about what, the words were indistinct and distant, as if heard from the far end of a large room. In the den, a lone child sat in front of the television, a girl Melissa didn't recognize, with short blonde hair and a hearing aid in her left ear. The TV had been turned up and the sound nearly drowned out the noise of the adults in the next room. Then he appeared through the sliding glass door that led into the room. Captain Ooze looked as hideous, perhaps more, than he had before. With those long fingers, he slowly opened the door, so quietly the young girl didn't notice. Again, Melissa tried to yell, but she had no voice and was forced to simply watch as Captain Ooze took two quick steps into the room, placed a hand on her mouth, grabbed her up and yanked her into the darkness.

Melissa awoke sweating and sobbing. She jumped out of bed and ran to her father's room, shaking him awake.

"What is it, darling?" he asked, his voice croaking from sleep and grabbing his glasses from the nightstand.

"I had a bad dream."

Walt had been through this before. After Joelle, his wife and her mother, died, Melissa was plagued by unsettling dreams. He had learned to be patient with these episodes, which had fortunately disappeared during in the past year. He knew to give her time to be quiet and gather herself. Sometimes she preferred to share the dream and other times she didn't. Dr. Bryant recommended just letting her share when she needed to.

She sat on the edge of the bed and he rubbed her coppery hair, waiting for her to calm down. But she didn't. The intensity of this one episode seemed to be stronger than all the others. Small tremors ran through her body.

"Captain Ooze," she whimpered.

"What's that, darling?"

"I saw Captain Ooze. In my dream."

"Captain Ooze?" he asked. *Why does that sound familiar?* he thought.

"He's from the sign I found down by the river. He looks like a pirate. Ugly and mean. And in my first dream I saw him take Hollis."

"You saw a picture of this character, Captain Ooze, and then dreamed he took away Hollis? That's understandable, dear. Sometimes our minds…"

"I saw him take away Hollis *before* I knew Hollis had disappeared. The same night. I didn't know he was taken until the next day"

Walt sat up, his body rigid now, listening carefully. He let her continue at her own pace. She explained her first dream, seeing Captain Ooze sneak up and snatch Hollis from his backyard, and then being afraid to tell anyone about it because she knew she had a habit of having bad dreams and didn't want to seem like a silly little girl. Walt took this all in calmly and gently.

"And what about tonight? What did you dream tonight?"

"I dreamed about a girl."

"Do you know her?"

"No. She was blonde, small. Maybe six or so. She had a hearing aid, I think, and was in a dirty house. Her parents were arguing in the next room while she was watching TV in the den. Then…" Melissa's voice faded and she began to tremble, tears filling her eyes. Walt just continued to rub her hair and give her time to collect herself. "…then I could hear Captain Ooze's wooden leg tapping outside and he came in through the sliding glass thingy and grabbed the little girl." She burst into tears and fell into her father's chest. He held her for twenty minutes, until the quaking sobs ended in small hiccups.

"Lissy, there are any number of reasons this could have happened. You saw this picture that frightened you and happened to dream about this boy you know getting taken by him. I know it seems unlikely, but I guarantee you there's no connection. And then you got so worked about it that your brain, which can sometimes be a strange part of us, made up a new bad dream for you. That's all it is, though. There's no connection."

"You mean there's no Captain Ooze?"

"No. He's not real. He's just a drawing."

"And he didn't take a little girl tonight."

"No."

She smiled through red eyes.

"Do you want to go back to your bed or would you like to sleep here?" he asked.

She paused.

"I think I'll go back to my room."

"Okay. Well, remember that you're safe and I'm here."

Cheeks still flushed from crying, she smiled and rubbed away the last of the tears.

"Sleep well, darling."

"Right-er-roo, Daddy," she said, somewhat unconvincingly, and tottered back toward her room.

‡

The next Amber Alert came at 9:45 a.m. the next morning. Walt was mowing the lawn while Melissa read a book on the front porch. His cellphone squelched. He killed the lawn mower engine and and clicked the alert. Abigail Litwell, age seven, disappeared from her home the night before. The accompanying picture showed a small, smiling girl with short blonde hair. The alert mentioned she wore a hearing aid. A chill went through his veins and he looked over at his daughter, calmly reading.

"Lissy!"

She looked up. "Yes, Daddy?"

"Can you show me that sign you found? The one with Captain Ooze?"

Sensing the strange energy coming from her dad, Melissa asked if something was wrong, but Walt said everything was going to be okay, she just needed to show him the sign first. They drove to the restaurant and walked through the back lot to the sand bank. She clung to her father's waist and pointed.

"There it is."

The corner of the sign was still sticking out of the sandbank. Captain Ooze was clearly visible.

"Wait here, honey," Walt said. But Melissa didn't let go.

"Don't leave me alone up here."

"It'll be just a second."

"No, Daddy."

"Okay… follow me and be careful."

Walt held Melissa's hand and together they awkwardly made their way down the slope toward the sign.

When they reached it, Melissa hid behind her dad as he examined the visible bit.

"Stand back a little, Lissy."

Melissa took a couple of steps away and Walt grabbed the corner of the sign and pulled, rocking as he did so. The sign was deeply lodged, but slowly it began to pull away, revealing the rest. Red and sweaty, Walt finally freed the entire sign — all six-by-eight feet of it. Sand and dirt caked the sign so he pushed it a few feet down into the river and washed it off.

On the top of the sign, in script, were the words "RealKleen Defeats Ooze Every Time". On a field of golden yellow, an enormous lantern-jawed figure, wearing a navy-blue bicorne, waistcoat with gold epaulettes and piping and carrying a scabbard, towered over Captain Ooze who cowered beneath him. His name, the sign revealed, was Admiral RealKleen. He had a large drooping mustache, shoulder length blonde hair, and absurdly large barrel chest.

Upon seeing the sign, Walt had a quick flashback to his childhood, to the commercials he saw for RealKleen soap, which featured these two characters. He recalled that the two would engage in naval battles where Admiral RealKleen always wound up sinking Captain Ooze. The RealKleen soap company must have gone out of business long ago and this sign must have been buried for decades. But what had this to do with Melissa's nightmares and the missing children?

"Daddy, he…he kind of looks like you," she said, having dared to open her eyes and look at the sign. She was talking about Admiral RealKleen. Walt nodded and had to admit that, yes he did more than slightly resemble the character. The quiver was gone from her voice now. A new resolve seems to have replaced it. Something about seeing Admiral RealKleen seemed to reduce her fear.

"Was another child taken?" she said, finally asking the question she had been afraid to ask since the arrived.

Walt never lied to Melissa and didn't plan to start. "Yes, honey. Her name is Abigail Litwell. She's from Duncanville and looks like the girl you described in your dream."

"Can I see her picture?"

Walt pulled out his phone and showed her.

"That's her. That's the girl I saw." She looked up. "What does it mean? Why am I seeing them? Why am I seeing Captain Ooze?"

"I don't know," he said, feeling a similar anguish to the time he had to try to explain to four-year-old Melissa why her mom wouldn't be coming home from the hospital. He felt impotent in the face of whatever was happening, as if he was standing two inches from an enormous picture and couldn't see the whole of the image. In that moment, too, he felt an deep gratitude for Melissa's existence and pulled her close. He knew, whatever this was, he wasn't going to allow anything to take her away.

Walt was unsure of what to do now. Was it possible Captain Ooze was really the cause of these disappearances? That his daughter was actually dreaming reality? He absolutely couldn't deny that she had seemingly dreamt Abigail's disappearance, a girl who lived ten miles away and she almost certainly had never met. Somewhere, deep in Walt's heart, he understood that something terrible and strange was happening and it seemed to be connected to his daughter and this sign, this ridiculous drawing of a cartoon pirate. If he was hearing about this and not living it, he would have laughed. But instead, as he and Melissa headed back to the car, he had to keep his hands in his pockets so she wouldn't see them shaking.

‡

A week went by and Abigail and Hollis remained missing. FBI agents had been called in and news vans from Detroit and Chicago were stationed outside the tiny Martel County Sheriff's Department. The water level also broke another record and the Larson Yacht Club (really a glorified double-wide) fell into the marina after the dune it perched on eroded away.

Melissa went to bed that Thursday night as she normally did, around ten, after helping her dad close up the restaurant at nine. She brushed her teeth and went to the den to tell him good night as he watched the evening news to catch up on the latest developments with the missing children. Janet Arnez from WBLP was sticking a microphone in Sheriff DeRey's weary face. *The men and women on the force are working day and night to help get those children back home. We are also grateful to the FBI for providing us with…*

"Night, Daddy."

"Night, Lissy." She kissed him the top of his shiny head and went back to her room.

She settled into her bed, the dappled shadows cast on the wall by the streetlight no longer scaring her as they had when she was five and six. She was so relaxed that she didn't even sense herself slipping into sleep before finding herself in her den, still wearing her nightgown.

The lights were off. Her father had gone to bed. She could even see from the clock on the bookshelf that it was 1:32 a.m. Was she sleepwalking? She felt as if she were moving through water. She heard before she saw. The arrhythmic *thud, thud.*

She turned and saw a dark figure passing between the shadows. It was Captain Ooze, there was no doubt; she could tell even in the dark. She could smell him, the reek of bad water and rotting wood. She wanted to run, but she couldn't. She could only watch as he slowly made his way toward her, then past her and down the hall to her room. Where was her dad? Why didn't he wake up? She struggled to follow him, to scream, to do anything. She saw him open her bedroom door and could even, from the den, see herself in her bed, a small lump under the covers. Captain Ooze reached down and quietly picked up her limp body out of bed. Summoning all her strength, she tried to scream "Wake up!" but, again, her voice was trapped.

Suddenly she was in blackness, a blackness pure and suffocating. She tried to move but she couldn't. She screamed but her voice was swallowed up by the dark. And all around her, she sensed the creaking of heavy timbers and the slow heaving of water.

‡

Walt had a morning ritual. He always awoke promptly at seven, poured himself his one and only cup of coffee and began putting breakfast together, often quickly assembled from choice leftovers from the restaurant the night before. Then he would wake Melissa up at around 7:30.

On this morning, he made whitefish on toast with home fries and poached eggs while he listened to updates about the missing children on the radio. He felt a parent's anguish at their loss but also a twinge of gratitude that his own child was sleeping safely in her room. At 7:35, while two plates steamed on the kitchen table, Walt went to Melissa's room and knocked on the door.

"Lissy, it's time to wake up."

He pushed her door open slightly and peered in. The empty unmade bed did not fully register at first. It was like hearing someone mispronounce a familiar word. He threw aside the covers to be sure, then tore through the rest of the house yelling her name, opening every door, looking behind and beneath every piece of furniture. His heart wanted to leap out of his chest and go find her.

As soon as he had exhausted every possibility, extinguished every hope that she might crawl out from a cabinet with a smile on her face and yell "Boo!" he called the police. The first policeman arrived four minutes later, the rest soon followed and by 8:10, his house was swarming with law enforcement. The men in the suits, the detectives, tried to be gentle but they had a job to do, so they peppered him with usual questions about the last time he had seen her, what they had eaten for dinner, if she had any relatives who might want to take her, who her close friends were...

He decided not to mention the dreams or the sign or Captain Ooze as he knew it would be dismissed instantly as the gibbering of a grief-dazed father.

By then the news had arrived, vans clogging the streets, their satellite dishes eagerly beaming information about the fresh tragedy.

Walt began to get up, pushing the detectives out of the way.

"I can't just sit here! I've got to go look! She's out there somewhere. Someone's got her."

The stoutest of the detectives placed his hand on Walt's shoulder and urged him back down.

"We're working on it, Mr. Yancey. We'll do everything we can to locate your daughter," he said, with the gentle banality of a bored priest.

From his front porch, Walt gazed out at the chaos of yellow cordon tape and flashing lights and people he knew and didn't know standing at the edges of his yard, gazing on him with pity and curiosity, the same way, he realized, he had looked at the other parents of the missing kids.

Then for the briefest of moments, as small as the distance of time between two thoughts, he saw him, Captain Ooze, crouching low and peering from behind one of the news vans. He looked as close to the drawing of him as reality allowed, the same sallow, sunken face, the same bulging eyes, the greasy hair pulled back into a ratty ponytail. His face was contorted into a hideous grin and his long fingers curled around the van's bumper.

Almost as soon as he saw him, though, he was gone. Walt ran down the steps and over to the van. He looked underneath. Nothing. He tore through the crowd of people, trying to locate him, trying to see him. There was nowhere for him to have gone. He knew everyone was staring at him, but he didn't care. A cocktail of adrenaline and grief was carrying him along, but Captain Ooze was simply not there.

‡

Weeks passed. The news vans were the first to leave, and soon all the parents whose children were safe began letting them play out until evening again. Every lead was was pursued, every potential sighting followed up. But soon these trickled away. The cops stopped calling. Missing posters with Melissa's picture and information that had been stapled to telephone poles and placed on bulletin boards inside grocery stores and gas station entrances soon decayed in the rain or were eventually pulled down and replaced. And still the waters rose.

Initially, Walt leaned on the Terry and Litwell families for comfort and support. They were the only ones whom he felt free to talk to, but even they eventually stopped returning his calls after he mentioned his theory about Captain Ooze. By Halloween, he no longer had the energy to dedicate to the restaurant and he closed it permanently.

One morning in early November, when the days were growing short and cold, Walt hauled the RealKleen sign up the bank using the wench on his truck and took it to his garage where he studied it, searching it for answers. Surely there was meaning to be found, the universe had to

cough up a solution. He researched the RealKleen company, based in
Chicago from 1956 to 1972 until they went bankrupt. He found
advertisements in old newspapers which he would clip and collect in a
folder. On some internet message boards, he found a couple of references
to the Captain Ooze from the RealKleen commercials.

```
Greenboy219:  Anybody remember that creepy
              commercial from the late 60's
              featuring that really scary
              pirate guy? I think it was for
              a cleaning company

Dalek4Life:   Yes! I know what you're talking
              about he had those bug eyes!

Heeleeum:     He was called Captain Ooze, I
              think

Greenboy219:  That's right! Captain Ooze! He
              gave me nightmares!
```

That was the most-detailed mention of Captain Ooze he could find
anywhere.

He finally managed to get a hold of a VHS copy of one of the
commercials from the early 70's. A crudely designed website listed it in
an enormous archive of old television commercials available for
purchase.

It arrived in a simple brown paper parcel with his name and address
handwritten in felt-tip pen. Walt found his old VCR in the attic.
Miraculously, it still worked. He put the tape in and pressed 'play.' The
tape began.

After a few moments of shaky blackness, through the warping sine
waves of distortion, static and washed out colors, a synthesizer played a

kind of sea shanty. On simply drawn curls of blue waves and white foam bobbed a boat flying the Jolly Roger. In the distance was a small knot of ships.

"Shiver me timbers, ye swabs!" a wheezy voice cried out followed by laughter. "Today we shall attack the Dinner Plate Armada."

Walt had not remembered the voice but the neural pathway that held that memory suddenly lit up, glowing hot with remembrance.

The commercial cut to a shot of the deck of the boat. Captain Ooze hunched on the bow, one hand on the wheel, much as he had looked when Walt had seen him by the van. His crew of three small figures in striped shirts faced him, their backs to the viewer. Walt leaned in, touching his hand to the screen. One crew member had short blonde hair like Abigail, the other had brown hair like Hollis and the figure on the right had long red hair pulled into a ponytail, just like Melissa. *Show me her face,* he thought. *Please just show me.*

"They'll be no match for my Grease Canon!"

Captain Ooze pulled the sheet off the object next to him, a black cannon conveniently labeled "Grease". The crew, backs still turned, cheered.

"Ready the cannon!" he wheezed.

"Right-er-roo, Captain Ooze!" the small, red-headed figure said.

Walt sat straight up in his chair and rewound the tape, listening again.

"Right-er-roo, Captain Ooze!"

It's her voice. Oh God, it's her voice.

He allowed the commercial to finish.

The cannon fired a blob of grease which arced, then split apart and showered the other ships with a slimy rain. Captain Ooze did a small jig to celebrate, cackling with joy.

A triumphant melody played as a bigger frigate appeared on the horizon.

"Not this time, you scourge!" boomed a man's clear, deep voice.

And instantly Admiral RealKleen, with his large chest and sparkling uniform, was upon Captain Ooze's ship.

With a blast from his canon — this one labeled "RealKleen Detergent" — Admiral RealKleen sank Captain Ooze's ship.

The announcer then proclaimed: "RealKleen defeats Ooze, every time!"

Captain Ooze and his crew, clinging to boards, floated off to the horizon and the commercial faded out. That was it. There was nothing more on the tape. He switched off the television.

For minutes, hours perhaps, he sat alone in the quiet dark of the garage. In his soul he felt the terror of endless free fall, the terminal velocity of despair.

But finally, he did the only thing there was to do: rewind and watch the tape again.

And again, and again…

"Not this time, you scourge," he whispered like a prayer.

James Hadley Griffin is a teacher and writer living in Alabama with his wife and two hounds. At one time or another, he has lived in most of the Southern capitals. His fiction has appeared in Ellery Queen's Mystery Magazine, Tough, Shotgun Honey, Popcorn Fiction, and Pulp Modern Flash.

I Hear You Paint Portraits

Keith J. Hoskins

Thomas Doyle positioned a fresh canvas on the waiting easel. Retrieving his newly cleaned brushes, he carefully arranged them on the tray beside his array of paints. He glanced upward and sensed the lights were a tad too harsh, prompting him to walk over to the control panel and adjust the dimmer to a more suitable setting. Taking a deep breath, he nodded in reassurance. Everything was in place; he was ready.

Through the thin curtain veil on the studio door's window, Thomas caught sight of a woman's silhouette. A gentle tap resounded on one of the panes, prompting him to turn the deadbolt and cautiously swing open the door.

"May I help you?" he said with an ingratiating smile.

"Good morning." Her voice was weak, as was the smile she returned. "I hear you paint portraits."

"Mrs. Whitmire?"

"Yes. I hope I'm not too early."

"Not at all. Please, come in." Thomas gestured for her to enter, then he closed and locked the door once she was inside.

The older woman took slow, careful steps as she proceeded deeper into the modest studio. She stopped when she noticed the blank canvas spotlighted from above, awaiting its master's touch.

"Is everything okay?" asked Thomas.

Startled, she looked at him apologetically. "I'm sorry. Yes. Where would you like me?"

"Well, I have several different seating options for you. I have a chaise, a wingback chair, an easy chair …" Thomas pointed to the various pieces of furniture around the open room; the choices seemed overwhelming for the woman.

"The wingback looks nice, I suppose."

"Good choice," said Thomas, then he proceeded to carry the chair to the open spot next to his easel.

"Is what I'm wearing appropriate?" she asked.

Thomas regarded her royal-blue dress trimmed with white lace and smiled.

"I think it's perfect," he told her. "The color matches your eyes."

"It's my husband's favorite."

"Please." He gestured for her to sit.

The old woman took her seat and let Thomas adjust her so that she was presented at the most optimal angle without being too uncomfortable to hold for an extended period.

"Let's begin," he said, giving her a comforting smile and pat on the hand. She nodded, and he took his place in front of the expanse of white. Taking up a brush, he selected the first color to dab onto his palette.

Thomas, like many painters, preferred to work back to front. He used a neutral hue for the backdrop, something to give the location some ambiguity. He would then begin to frame out the chair with a moderate amount of detail. He didn't want to waste time with the frivolities.

Despite his considerable talent as an artist, the subject demanded an otherworldly focus. He had to unlock the hidden life force within her, transcending ordinary brushstrokes. It wasn't merely capturing her essence; he felt an inexplicable need to seize her very soul, an unseen power guiding his hand. The eyes held an eerie significance; they were the windows to a world beyond, bestowing a mystical aura upon the artwork he was creating.

Upon completion, he took a step back and gazed at his creation with a mixture of satisfaction and trepidation. It was more than good; it was mesmerizing, almost alive. He sensed he had achieved what he set out to do, fulfilling the desperate need of the elderly, infirm woman in the chair six feet away.

He glanced up at the clock on the wall. Its hands showed a quarter past two in the afternoon. More than four hours had transpired. But to Thomas ... an hour, a day ... it was all the same when he crafted these portraits. Time seemed almost as malleable as the paints he used.

"Are you done?" Mrs. Whitmire asked. She looked tired, justifiably so.

"Yes. Would you like to see it?"

With Thomas's gentle support, she gracefully unfolded from the chair. Taking her hand, he guided her toward the easel's front. As her eyes beheld his creation, a subtle metamorphosis seemed to wash over Mrs. Whitmire. Her posture straightened, and the burden in her eyes lifted, almost imperceptibly. It was as though the painting's enchantment forged a profound connection with its subject. And in that poignant moment, like all the others before, Thomas realized that she knew—truly knew—the mysterious power the artwork held over her.

"When will … when can I …"

"You can pick the painting up on Wednesday."

"That soon?"

"I can postpone it a bit if you'd like."

"No. Wednesday will be good. That'll be fine."

"Very good. Would you like me to call you a cab?"

"Could you call my husband? He can pick me up."

"Certainly."

"Oh, what about payment?"

"Your husband can pay me on Wednesday."

Twenty minutes later, Mrs. Jean Ann Whitmire stepped into her husband's Continental and vanished into the afternoon, leaving behind her portrait in the care of a man burdened by a weight that threatened to crush him like a mere paper cup.

After placing Mrs. Whitmire's painting on the shelf, Thomas went to the studio fridge, took out a beer, and downed half the bottle before pausing to reflect on the freshly painted work before him.

"Damn it," he cursed, then turned away and hurled the bottle against the brick wall, sending glass and beer in all directions.

He spent the next couple of hours cleaning up the studio, then he went upstairs to his apartment and took a shower. Afterward, he started dinner; his wife, Lara, would be home by six.

‡

"Did your appointment show today?" asked Lara.

Thomas had prepared spaghetti and meat sauce, with garlic bread on the side. They cherished their evening ritual of sharing their day's highlights, as they did every weeknight. Lara, however, rarely asked about Thomas's clients. She usually let him broach the subject. Thus, when she unexpectedly inquired, it caught him off guard.

"Yes. Mrs. Whitmire."

"How did it go?"

"It was … okay." Thomas absentmindedly twirled pasta on his fork, then he dumped it on the plate and started again.

"Just okay?"

"You know how these things go."

"I do, but, try not to dwell on it. That's not good for you."

"I'll try."

Her silence made him look up; her worried expression made him give her a placating smile.

"I won't dwell on it. I promise."

But he did.

‡

Wednesday came and Thomas had dinner waiting when Lara came home. As the couple ate, Lara dominated the conversation, reiterating her day's hell.

When an uncomfortable silence ensued, she said, "Everything okay with you? How was your day?"

"Mr. Whitmire came by and picked up his wife's portrait. She passed early this morning."

"That's what's supposed to happen, right?"

"Yeah, but..." He paused, struggling to find the right words. "He was pretty shaken up. It was all I could do to hold it together myself."
Her eyes softened with understanding, but her jaw tightened to reaffirm her position. "Did he pay you?"

"Yeah, he paid me. That's not the point. The point is—"

"—The point is you provide a service that no one else can. You prevent a lot of suffering for your subjects as well as their families. And the burden you carry takes a toll on you. I see it every time. So, you need to be compensated for your sacrifice and talent."

"Talent? What talent? I just paint them and ... you know."

"Yes, I do know. And I think it's remarkable. Some would say that you're doing God's work, Thomas."

"Sometimes it feels more like the Devil's work."

Lara sighed. "Do you have a class tomorrow morning?"

"Yeah, nine to noon."

"Just focus on your students. Teaching is good work too," she said, trying to offer him a glimmer of solace amidst the weight of his responsibilities.

He nodded. "I will."

"You know," Lara said as she refilled her wine glass, "you can stop whenever you want to. The money isn't that important. I'm sorry if that's how it sounded."

"I know," he replied as he took the bottle from her and filled his own glass. "But the work is."

‡

The next morning, his class was its usual bright point of the week and a distraction from the world. When the class ended, the students filed out of the studio, chatting in their various groups about their art, weekend plans, and where they were going for lunch.

Amidst their excited prattle, Thomas couldn't help but smile, and once the last few had left, he closed and locked the door behind them. When he turned back to the studio, a couple of knocks on the door told him a student most likely had forgotten something and doubled back.

But when he opened the door, an older man in a suede coat and fedora stood in the frame, slightly hunched, and grasping a handkerchief in a hand adorned with liver spots revealing the weight of time on him. His gaunt face hosted eyes that pleaded with desperation, his stained teeth and lips revealed a lifetime of smoking.

"May I help you, sir?" Thomas asked.

"Yes, I—"

The old man was suddenly overcome with a violent cough that echoed with the unmistakable grip of disease. He covered his mouth with the handkerchief, struggling to contain the relentless fit. When the coughing subsided, he withdrew his hand, revealing fresh crimson stains on the once-pristine linen.

"I'm sorry," he said with a raspy voice. He met Thomas's eyes and added, "I ... I hear you paint portraits."

"Yes, I do," Thomas replied, slowly and confused. "But I don't usually have walk-ins. How did you hear about me?"

"Jack Whitmire gave me your address. He said you were able to help his wife."

Thomas understood and nodded. "Please, come in, Mr. ..."

The old man shuffled inside and began to take off his coat and hat. "Lomax. Ed Lomax."

"Here," said Thomas, "let me take those for you, Mr. Lomax." He took the garments and hung them on a nearby coat rack. "So, how do you know Mr. Whitmire?"

"He's my next-door neighbor. Our families have been friends for thirty years."

"I see. And you do know what it is I do here?"

"Yes. But, tell me, is it true?"

"I'm afraid it is."

"Then, my dear man, you are a godsend."

Thomas smiled at the ironic compliment. "Let me gather my tools and we can begin."

The next few hours whisked away in a blur as Thomas immersed himself in painting the man's image, surrendering to the mysterious forces that guided his hand. When at last he completed the portrait, he turned the easel around, presenting Mr. Lomax with the finished work to judge.

"It's amazing. It's wonderful and terrifying at the same time. It feels like I'm looking at me, yet not me. Does that make any sense?"

"I think so," Thomas replied.

"What happens now?"

"Someone needs to pick up the painting on a day of my choosing. With today being Thursday, does Monday work for you? That'll give you the weekend to do whatever you need to do."

"That'll be fine. Do I pay you now?"

"Usually, the person who picks it up pays. Who will that be?"

"My son-in-law. I'll make sure he takes care of everything. How much will he need to bring?"

"I tell people to pay what they feel the service is worth."
"I understand."

"Do you need a ride home?" Thomas offered.

"No. I'm parked out on the street. I'll be fine."

Thomas helped the man with his coat and hat before assisting him to the door. As Ed Lomax prepared to exit the studio, he turned back to Thomas, his eyes reflecting gratitude.

"God bless you, young man," he said warmly.

"You as well, Mr. Lomax," Thomas replied with a genuine smile, touched by the old man's heartfelt words. Words he needed to hear.

‡

On Monday, just before noon, a harsh knock rattled the door of the studio. Thomas opened the door to reveal a middle-aged man clad in a tie and suit jacket. His stoic face was unreadable; the badge on his belt was not.

"Good morning," said Thomas as he felt the blood rush to his face. "May I help you?"

"I'm Detective Frank Romine …"

Those words sent Thomas teetering on the precipice of panic.

"… I'm here to pick up my father-in-law's portrait."

Relief enveloped Thomas, smothering his anxiety. For now.

"Please, Detective. Come in."

"You can call me Frank. I'm not here in an official capacity. I don't know why I announced myself like that. Habit, I suppose."

Thomas closed the door as the man walked inside, his head slowly pivoting as he took in the studio.

"Let me grab Mr. Lomax's portrait." Thomas walked to the back and grabbed the painting off the shelf.

"Nice place you have here. Been doing this a long time?"

"About ten years, or so."

"You teach art?" Romine asked after noticing the score of easels along the side wall.

"Yes. Tuesdays and Thursdays. Are you interested?"

"Me? Dear Lord, no. I have enough trouble with stick figures."

"Here it is. Sorry it's not wrapped. I was about to do so when you knocked."

"That's fine. Oh, he wanted me to give you this." Romine reached into his breast pocket, removed an envelope, then handed it to Thomas.

"Thank you." Thomas slipped the envelope into his back pocket and started for the studio entrance. "Here, let me get the door for you.

The detective pivoted but did not take a step. "Aren't you going to ask me how my father-in-law is doing?"

Thomas swallowed. "How is Mr. Lomax? I know he wasn't feeling well."

"He's dead."

"Oh? I'm so sorry to hear that."

"Passed away this morning. We knew he had little time left—lung cancer, small cell—but we didn't think he'd leave us so soon."

"I guess it was his time."

"That's what I told my wife, but the strange thing is, the last thing he told me was that I had to stop by here and pick up this portrait. He was quite insistent. He gave me the envelope and made me promise to pick it up today. It was as if he knew he was going to die."

"Perhaps a man in his condition feels like every day could be his last."

"Perhaps." Romine held the painting at arm's length and examined it from top to bottom. "Amazing work, Mr. Doyle. I haven't seen him look this good in years."

"Thank you," said Thomas, still lingering by the door. "I try to capture his life essence. What he looks like on the inside, more than just his physical appearance."

"Well, you did an amazing job. My wife will be grateful for this." Thomas reached for the door's handle.

"Funny thing," Romine said, still looking at the portrait. "Last week we took him to the viewing for his neighbor, Mrs. Whitmire. Nice lady, apparently lifelong friends. Anyway, on display, next to her casket, was a portrait of her that looked a lot like the style of this one. Did you know Mrs. Whitmire?"

"Ah, yes. She was a client of mine. I painted her portrait about a week ago."

"Exactly a week ago. Then she died on Wednesday morning. Her viewing was Friday, then her funeral was Saturday. My father-in-law sees you on Thursday, spends the weekend making plans and finalizing things—including having me pick up this portrait, then he passes this morning."

"I'm not sure what you're saying, Mr. Romine."

"I'm saying this is a huge coincidence, and in my line of work, we don't like coincidences."

"What line of work is that?" came a woman's voice.

Both men turned to the back of the studio where Lara stood at the top of the stairs next to their apartment door.

"Hi, honey," Thomas said, both surprised and relieved at her timely appearance. "This is Ed Lomax's son-in-law, Detective Frank Romine." Lara descended the stairs and walked confidently toward the two men.

"Picking up Mr. Lomax's portrait, I see," she said.

Before Romine could speak, Thomas added, "Mr. Lomax passed earlier this morning."

"Oh, I'm terribly sorry to hear that. My condolences."

"Thank you, ma'am."

"Was there anything else, Detective? I know this must be a very trying day for you and your family."

"No, ma'am. I was just leaving." He started for the door then stopped. "Actually, there is one more thing. I couldn't help but take a peek inside that envelope I handed you, Mr. Doyle. And I saw a check for ten grand made out to you. Now, I don't know much about art, but that seems like a lot of money for a painting done by a relatively unknown artist. I mean, it's a wonderful work of art, but ten grand …? Do you normally charge that much for a painting?"

"I usually ask the subject to pay what they can," said Thomas, "what they feel the painting's worth to them."

"And you're saying my father-in-law felt this was worth ten thousand dollars."

"Apparently so."

"And what about Mrs. Whitmire? How much did she pay for her portrait?"

"That, Mr. Romine, is none of your business," said Lara. "I'm sorry if you're not happy with the price of the painting, but that is a business deal done between Mr. Lomax and my husband. So, if there is nothing else, I must ask you to leave."

Romine smiled; he knew he'd been put in check. He nodded farewell to them both.

Thomas held the door open for the detective then quickly shut it when he departed.

Thomas turned to his wife. "Of course, Mr. Lomax's son-in-law had to be a detective."

"Doesn't matter. He can be suspicious all he wants; he won't find anything. Nothing except a very talented man."

"I hope you're right."

"Of course, I'm right. The truth is too outlandish for anyone to believe."

Lara wrapped her arms around Thomas's neck, igniting a passionate kiss that eclipsed any they'd shared in ages. He reciprocated her affection, mirroring her fervor with equal intensity. However, a desperate knock on the door compelled them to reluctantly separate.

Lara raised an eyebrow. "Do you think the good detective forgot something?"

"Let's find out." Thomas opened the door. A young woman stood in the frame, wide-eyed and pale. "Hello, miss. Were you looking to sign up for art lessons? Our next class is tomorrow—"

"No," she said. Her eyes flicked to Lara then back to Thomas. "I … I hear you paint portraits."

Thomas gave a muted chuckle thinking this must be a joke, but the unwavering gaze in the woman's eyes told him that she was quite serious.

"I'm sorry. You must have the wrong place." He started to close the door, but the woman blocked it with her foot and took a half-step inside.

"You are Thomas Doyle, aren't you?"

"Yes, but—"

"I was told to come see you. He told me you help people like me."

Thomas gave the woman a cursory glance; she looked healthy, in her late twenties. Not his normal clientele.

"I'm afraid you have the wrong guy. I don't help people like you."

"But I said the right phrase. Didn't I? Isn't that the password or something?"

Lara stepped forward and took the woman's arm. "Come inside, dear. Out of the cold."

Thomas knew that was a smart move on his wife's part to keep this conversation more private. He shut the door, turned the deadbolt, and then peeked through the curtain to be sure no one else lingered nearby.

"Who told you to say that?" Thomas demanded.

"Uh … Dr. Duvall. He said when people are out of options and they need the pain to end, you can help them find peace." Her eyes became glassy, and tears trickled down her cheek.

"Duvall sent you here? What exactly—" He cut himself off. He never inquired about a client's health issues, but he didn't feel comfortable letting this woman come into his studio without an appointment and looking, for the most part, healthy.

Did Romine send her here to fish information out of me? Was she wearing a wire?

"What's your name, dear?" Lara's voice interjected.

"Christine. Christine Filner, but everyone calls me Chrissy."

Lara tugged Thomas's arm and pulled him back a few steps.

"Hey," she whispered. "Let me call Dr. Duvall and see if he did send her."

Lara made her way to the rear of the studio, while Thomas guided the woman to a nearby chair.

"Please, have a seat, Chrissy," he offered and handed her a tissue.

"Thank you." She used the tissue to wipe her eyes and nose.

"Have you known Dr. Duvall long?"

"I've been seeing him for a few years. He's been … he's been very helpful." A fresh bout of tears welled up, prompting Thomas to offer another tissue.

"Oh, I'm sorry, but I don't have much money. I do have this, though. It belonged to my grandmother."

Chrissy fished something out of her pocket then presented it to Thomas. It was a gold ring with the largest diamond he had ever seen. On either side of the diamond were two rubies staring back at him like glowing red eyes.

"I'm sure this will be fine. Would you like some water?" he asked.

"Please. That would be great."

Thomas walked to the fridge and removed a bottle of water. As he did so, he shot Lara a glance, her cell phone up to her ear. She met Thomas's eyes and gave him a confirming nod.

Thomas smiled a thank you to his wife then walked back to the distraught woman and handed her the water.

"Okay, Chrissy," he sighed. "Are you ready to begin?"

‡

The next few days were relatively quiet for Thomas, including his Tuesday class. Even Lara had a good week at the courthouse, so their dinner conversations were more lighthearted than they had recently been. Thursday's class ended with its usual clamor, and as the students filed out of the studio, a familiar figure waited outside.

"Mr. Doyle," Detective Romine said. "Mind if I come in?"

Thomas hesitated for the briefest of moments before saying, "By all means, please."

Romine sauntered in and let his eyes scan the studio, this time as if with refreshed purpose. Once Thomas closed the door, the detective turned to face him.

"I'll get right to the point, Mr. Doyle. Do you know a girl named Christine Filner?"

Thomas considered lying to Romine, denying any knowledge of the woman, but he knew that the detective wouldn't be standing in his art studio if he didn't already know the answer.

"Yes. She was a client of mine. Why? Is she okay?"

"No, Mr. Doyle, she is not okay. She was found dead in her apartment yesterday morning, by her roommate."

"Oh my God. That's horrible."

"It is horrible," said Romine. "And such a shame for someone to die so young."

"Very true."

Thomas walked to the fridge and removed a beer. He made an offer to Romine who declined with a curt wave of his hand. Thomas opened the bottle and took a sip.

"I had a close friend growing up," Thomas said, "whose dad passed away at thirty-five from pancreatic cancer." He took a swig and shook his head. "I guess we never know when our time is up."

"That's very true, Mr. Doyle. However, Christine Filner wasn't sick. That's what's so baffling."

Thomas stopped the bottle inches from his mouth. "What do you mean?"

"I mean there was nothing physically wrong with her. She was as healthy as the proverbial horse."

"Are you certain? There had to be something wrong with her. Did you check with her doctor?"

"Oh, yes, we checked with Ms. Filner's doctor …" Romine removed a small notepad from his breast pocket and flipped through a few pages.

"... a Dr. Steven Duvall. But he hadn't seen her in months, almost a year. However, she had been seeing a psychiatrist quite regularly. Apparently, Ms. Filner was suffering from acute depression and on several medications for that. Medications that, apparently, she had stopped taking."

"Depression?" Thomas plopped onto the chaise and took a gulp of his beer.

"Funny thing is, her psychiatrist—are you ready for this—had a patient by the name of Jack Whitmire. The same Jack Whitmire whose wife had recently passed. A coincidence? Well, I don't have to tell you how I feel about coincidences. Do I?"

"It can't be," Thomas mumbled, hunched and dangling his bottle between his knees. She had to be sick. She had to. Lara called.

"So, how are you doing it, Mr. Doyle?"

"I'm sorry?" Thomas said, confused.

"The deaths. All three victims saw you just a few days before they checked out. The toxicology reports all came back clean. So, what is it, some exotic drug our doctors' tests can't pick up?"

"Detective, I assure you, I did nothing to those people except paint their portraits."

"Listen, Mr. Doyle, there have been three deaths within two weeks and all of them saw you shortly before they died. I'll get to the bottom of this. One way or another."

Thomas felt that this visit was more personal for Romine than professional. It was Romine's father-in-law that had passed, after all. Hell, he might not even be there on official police business.

"Are you charging me with anything, Detective Romine?"

"As of right now ... no. I don't have any concrete proof. Yet. But once I do—"

"Then I suggest you leave and return only when you've conjured up some imaginary charges. That is, of course, unless you ever want your portrait painted. I'd even do yours for free."

A glint in Romine's eyes suggested he understood the veiled threat, but it swiftly transformed into a more intense response.

"You hear me and hear me good," Romine retorted, jabbing a finger at Thomas's chest. "I *will* be back, and when I do, we'll have another conversation. Downtown. You got that?"

"I'll be waiting, Detective," Thomas responded evenly. He walked to the door, opened it, and with a gracious gesture, invited Romine to exit, a subtle smile playing on his lips.

Romine huffed, then briskly left the studio, with Thomas slamming the door closed behind him.

With the Detective gone, Thomas's smile vanished, and he pulled his cell phone from his pocket. He hit the call button next to Lara's name and waited for his wife to answer. After a couple of seconds, he said, "You need to come home, right now."

‡

Thomas was well into his sixth beer when the apartment door flung open. Lara burst in and hurried down the staircase to her husband who sat in the grip of the chaise with one leg drawn tightly against his chest.

"What's wrong, Thomas? What happened?"

"You lied to me." Thomas downed the rest of the bottle's contents then let it drop to the floor where it clanged against its companions.

"Are you drunk?"

"How observant."

"What's the matter? What happened?"

"You lied to me. That's what happened. You were supposed to call Dr. Duvall and ask him if he sent Chrissy to us."

"And I did. I—"

"Liar!" Thomas stood to level their gazes. "Detective Romine came by today. He said—well first he said Chrissy had died. But I knew that, didn't I? Then he tells me she wasn't sick. Not physically, anyway. Duvall told him he hadn't seen her in almost a year. But Romine did find out that she was seeing a shrink for depression and that she had stopped taking the meds prescribed by that shrink. Oh, and guess what … John Whitmire was seeing the same shrink. So you see, my dear wife, Chrissy wasn't sent here by Duvall. She must have been talking to Whitmire or overheard him talking to someone, or something like that. So then she comes in here, claiming Duvall sent her. And you were supposed to call Duvall and ask him, but you didn't. Did you? Why, Lara?" Thomas fell back into the chaise and began to sob into his hands. "Why, why, *why?*"

Lara lowered herself into the space next to Thomas. She placed her hand on his shoulder and said, "There was no answer when I called Duvall, and I could see Chrissy was desperate. I figured she had to be in a great deal of pain and that she couldn't be lying."

"Oh, but she was. She lied, and then you lied. Why would you do that? Did you see the ring she had for payment and know it was worth a shitload of money? Is that why?"

"You know that's not true. I would never do something like that for the money. I'm the one who told you to quit. Remember?"

"Yeah, I remember. But you knew I wouldn't quit. Feeling so damned righteous. Doing God's work, my ass."

"What do you want me to say, Thomas? I'm sorry? Well, I am. But now what? What do you want me to do?"

"I want you to go away. Just leave me alone."

Lara did as he demanded, leaving her husband to wallow in his self-pity and remorse.

‡

An insistent knocking reverberated through the studio. Each cadence becoming louder than the previous. When the door was finally opened, Detective Frank Romine stood in the egress.

"Good afternoon, Mrs. Doyle. Is your husband in?"

"Hello, Detective. No. I'm afraid he's not. Thomas passed away a few days ago. Heart attack."

"Oh. I'm so sorry to hear that. Did his family have a history of—"

"I don't know, Detective. All I know is that my husband is dead, and you were the last person to visit him. When I came home from work, he was quite upset by your conversation. I guess his heart couldn't take it."

"Um … I hope I …"

"Just leave, please, Mr. Romine. Unless your intention is to harass a grieving widow."

"No, ma'am. I'm sorry for your loss."

Lara shut the door in Romine's face.

She strode over to the easel, bathed in the eerie glow of the track lights, and removed the tarp shrouding the painting beneath. Her gaze fixated on the artwork for a moment, her lips curling into a sinister smile.

"Oh, Thomas," she hissed at the uncanny likeness of her late husband. "I'm almost impressed by your choice for an exit. Sad, but not entirely unexpected. You were always were expendable."

She continued, her voice dripping with malice. "Your void will be a mere inconvenience. It won't be long before I find a suitable replacement. I located you easily enough, after all."

Lara's fingers brushed against the painted lips, but her touch was far from affectionate. "Farewell, my dear," she whispered with a wicked grin. "You served your purpose, but I have a feeling that the best is yet to come."

Keith J. Hoskins is the author of seven short stories published in seven anthologies, his own anthology, and a trilogy of novellas. He is currently working on his first novel set in a fantasy world and a follow-up anthology of short stories.

Acknowledgements

We would like to extend a thank you to our previous guests and friends who encouraged us and blessed us with their time and talents. You all are what makes this writing gig so much fun.

From Nate:

On a more sentimental note, I would be remiss to neglect thanking my brother, James and his wife, Brianna who always encouraged me to write and read, even if it meant going some dark and twisted rabbit holes. To Travis Grundon, who published my first crime story in *Hoosier Noir* and has never failed to be a friend and supporter. To Big John, who has asked consistently about the podcast, and tolerated every long and winding speech about writing to which I've subjected him. And lastly, to my mother, who gave me her eyes for words and a heart that wants to understand people

From Kirstyn:

Thank you to Rijk van Zanten, for sharing your love and expertise on design and spreading the gospel of font selections.

To Steve Golds, for publishing my first story in *Punk Noir*.

To Rhiannon & Jamie Petras, for your proofreading talents and support.

To Rachel C., for making sure the correct people knew about this.

& To everyone who shared the word about this anthology. You are immensely appreciated.

Trigger Warnings

This is a collection of dark fiction stories, and as such, readers should expect stories with darkness in them, including, but not limited to, violence, manipulation, death, suffering, murder, and assault.

Outside of that, there are a few extra triggers listed here, for readers who wish to be aware of such content.

Pinkest Pink: Suicide

Polyptych of an Invisible Boy: Violence in a school setting

The Book of I: Death of parents, struggles with mental health, suicide

Two Day Rental: Sexual assault

Mouthfeel: Homophobia, suicide

I Hear You Paint Portraits: Suicide, assisted suicide

Printed in the USA
CPSIA information can be obtained
at www.ICGtesting.com
LVHW021410211223
766988LV00081B/3774